He Loved Her.

The thought came clear as the cry of a gull. He had been with many women since Beth had gone, and with each he had thought that he had made love, but that night with Danielle had brought back in a rush what he had been missing, what he had lost: the feel of two people who needed each other, who responded to each other, and who shared a passion that was overwhelming.

PAMELA FOXE
a versatile, prolific author, writes detective stories as well as adult and young adult fiction. For her material she draws on a lively imagination and a lifetime of traveling. She has lived in Singapore, Scotland, England, and California. Right now, she makes her home in the heart of Greenwich Village, New York.

Dear Reader:

Romance readers have been enthusiastic about Silhouette Special Editions for years. And that's not by accident: Special Editions were the first of their kind and continue to feature realistic stories with heightened romantic tension.

The longer stories, sophisticated style, greater sensual detail and variety that made Special Editions popular are the same elements that will make you want to read book after book.

We hope that you enjoy this Special Edition today, and will enjoy many more.

The Editors at Silhouette Books

PAMELA FOXE
Your Cheating Heart

Silhouette Special Edition
Published by Silhouette Books New York
America's Publisher of Contemporary Romance

Silhouette Books by Pamela Foxe

Your Cheating Heart (SE #216)

SILHOUETTE BOOKS

Distributed by Pocket Books

ISBN: 0-373-09005-6

First Silhouette Books printing January, 1985

10 9 8 7 6 5 4 3 2 1

Map by Ray Lundgren

America's Publisher of Contemporary Romance

Printed in the U.S.A.

BC91

For Alice and Michael

Your Cheating Heart

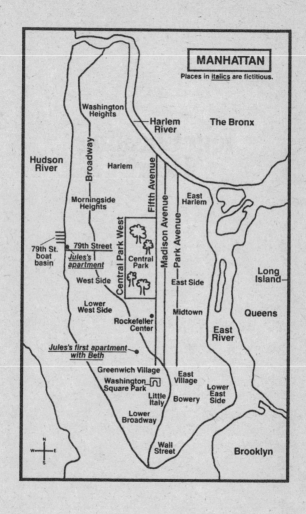

Chapter One

Jules Edwards ran a smooth path through the lather on his cheek. From the narrow bathroom window he had a view of the river beyond the Manhattan skyline, sparkling in the light of a fine September day. He thought how much he would rather be on the *Sapphire*, fighting the Atlantic waves on the way south to St. Thomas, than here facing what he had to do today. He had hired a crew of two, responsible boys from the Southampton Yacht Club, to take his thirty-eight-foot motor sailer south for the winter so he could use it when he had time, and he envied the boys the bright reflected light on the waves and the good strong wind in their sails that they would have today.

Instead, in his capacity as an attorney for the second largest record company in the world, it would be his unwelcome task today to read the riot act to a spoiled twenty-year-old rock singer who was eight months late in delivering a record. Jules had a pretty good idea what that would be like: the singer would be petulant, shocked at having to get out of bed before noon, and crying "artistic temperament." The manager, who would inevitably come along, would be obnoxious, condescending and dishonest.

Jules splashed cold water on his face, took a hand towel and wiped away the last of the lather. At thirty-four, he saw in the mirror a fine-looking man, six foot, thick brown hair with a gentle wave just showing gray at the temples, and bright gray eyes framed with the first of the squint lines that came from a summer of sailing. He smiled to remind himself that he had the life he wanted.

He threw the towel he wore about his waist into the corner. Seen naked, he still had an excellent body from playing tennis: darkly tanned, with broad shoulders and sturdy legs. He was vain enough to be watching for any signs of gray in the hair that matted his chest. So far there had been none. What's more, the dreaded middle-age spread that seemed to be creeping across the waists of all his married friends hadn't struck him yet. His midriff was as pebbled as when he left college, the thick mat of dark hair that covered his chest running in two straight lines down his rippled stomach.

In his bedroom, he threw the covers back over the high platform bed and began to lay out his clothes for the day: conservative, he decided. He'd show them, this child singer and the manager, that they were dealing with a hardheaded businessman. They'd better get this act together and start singing twelve tracks for a record or start looking for a hundred thousand dollars to return to Star Records. If they didn't deliver, Jules knew—and so would the boy's manager—his career was over. You only got one shot in the fast lane and you either came through or you dropped back with all the other hopefuls, thousands of them, who nearly reached the top but just didn't have what it took. They came year after year, like shoals of fish riding in on the tide, and a few, a very few, those with discipline as well as talent, made it. The rest . . . Jules knew what happened to the rest, and sometimes when he got calls at the office from desperate artists whom he'd dealt with years before it pained him. They never forgot that they had almost made it, never got over the dream that was almost theirs . . . and many of them had had real talent.

But talent wasn't enough, Jules reminded himself as he knotted the navy blue tie with the tiny white pindots. You had to have discipline too. For every talented singer who couldn't deliver there were a thousand waiting, ready to step into his place.

He took his double-breasted navy blazer off the hanger, threw it over his arm and went out into the living room to leave a note for Martha, his housekeeper, who came in every day to clean up and leave a meal in the oven to be warmed up if he got home late. Most nights he ate with clients, but sometimes he cleared his calendar and gave himself the rare pleasure of a night at home alone. From the large masculine living room he now stood in, he had a clear view down the Hudson River to the Statue of Liberty at the mouth of the harbor.

He had had the apartment entirely redone after Beth left, shipping off to auction all the country antiques that they had started to collect together. Now the corner room with the long windows that looked down upon the river was wall to wall in a soft gray carpet, the long curved sofa in front of the fire was a darker gray leather, the bookshelves rising along the walls were filled only with books he had collected in the last five years.

"Flowers!" he wrote to Martha. "Mums!" For he liked to have fresh flowers in all the rooms. He shrugged into his jacket, picked up the briefcase from his desk, where he had been reviewing the terms of the contract, and went out into the hall, closing the door behind him.

He liked living in this building. He was a private man and people here left you alone. He seldom met any of his neighbors, and that was the way he liked it.

He pressed the button for the elevator and stood humming to himself, thinking about the meeting ahead. His neighbor's newspaper was lying there outside the door and he ran his eye over the headline. His eyes stopped. "Rock Star," the headline read exactly where the paper was folded. Jules reached down, lifted the paper to look at the second part of the headline, and as he did so, the door opened.

His eyes were level with two slim legs peeking out of a champagne silk housecoat. As he stood, his gaze followed the line of the housecoat up past rounded hips, a small waist, breasts that he had to avoid staring at as they swelled under the silk, to two glaring green eyes in an angry face framed by thick dark hair that fell to the shoulders.

Jules could already feel the blood racing to his face in embarrassment.

"So you're the one who's been stealing my paper," the apparition in the silk robe said, reaching out and taking the paper forcefully from his hand.

"I saw the headline . . . ," Jules began in embarrassment.

"Buy your own paper!" the girl said.

"I wasn't . . . ," Jules tried to explain.

"They cost thirty cents, cheapskate!" she said, and the door slammed in his face.

Jules seemed to have lost his breath. He stood facing the door, which was inches from his face, burning with emotion that was as much anger as embarrassment.

New York! he thought.

He raised his fist to hammer on the door, intending to give her a lesson in manners, but the elevator door opened with a soft swoosh behind him and he turned and got in. As he rode down he had another vision of two blazing green eyes and a lush fall of dark curls. He drew a deep breath and calmed himself for the day ahead.

"Morning, Mr. Edwards," the doorman said as Jules strode across the vast high-ceilinged lobby. The building had been built in the thirties, when architecture was designed for people who expected space and air, unlike the new buildings with their tiny ratlike apartments and narrow, mean entrances. The lobby had marble floors, a Persian carpet and brass-framed windows. The front door, which Henry, the doorman, now held open for Jules, rose twelve feet up to a beautiful Art Deco window that on sunny days like this threw a rainbow of pastel light into the lobby.

"Morning, Henry," Jules said. "Fine day."

He stepped out into one of those mornings that reminded him why he tolerated the many difficulties of living in New York. Star Records paid him handsomely to act as their in-house counsel, and he was considered by his peers to be one of the finest entertainment lawyers in the business. As such, he got offers monthly from other record companies, most of them on the West Coast, where the center of the business was still located. But on a morning like this he felt a rising happiness at the sheer variety of New York, the seasons, the people, the far-off unseen hum of energy.

He turned up toward Broadway to catch a cab, breathing in the early-fall air with just a nip of the winter yet to come. The first of the leaves shuffled along the sidewalk, gold and yellow, pushed by a caressing autumn wind.

The memory of the door slammed in his

face subsided as he strode along past the
sidewalk vendors already laying out their
displays of bright scarves and handbags,
umbrellas, radios, everything that they had
somehow managed to obtain down on the
waterfront. These days the sidewalks of
New York looked as crowded and turbulent
as any Middle Eastern bazaar.

Jules raised his arm to flag down one of
the old Checker cabs. When he was settled
in the roomy interior, he began to rehearse
in his mind the late-morning meeting. Artists were like children, he knew, and had to
be treated with a mixture of indulgence and
discipline. Talent sprang from some mysterious source, like water deep in the earth,
and to bring it pure and clear to the surface
required careful management. But the record business was also one of the most
intrigue-ridden businesses in the world.
Huge fortunes were made and lost in one
season. Talent, however rare, had to take
second place to the balance sheet.

Jules sighed, not enjoying what was
ahead on this fine day where people outside
the cab window strode with such renewed
energy that you could practically see their
determination to succeed.

With the cab stalled in traffic at Columbus Circle, he opened his briefcase on his
lap and took out the contract with the sing-

er. It called for a two-record deal, and the first record had been a success, rising to the charts in its first week. *Variety,* the show business magazine, had put a bullet by the title *Honky-Tonk Hero* when it first appeared, which meant they predicted it would zoom upward, and it had. The lead single had taken off by itself and sold a million records, turning it gold. The voice, as he remembered it, was that of a husky young man. Looking at his background notes now, he saw that the boy had been eighteen when his record took off two years ago, catapulting him to national stardom. The record company had backed a nationwide tour, hoping that they had one of the great talents. The sad truth was that so many of the youngsters who hit it big didn't have the stamina to go the whole way, and they faded back into some place of lost hopes and dreams.

This one, Jules reflected, snapping his briefcase shut, was probably one of them. Tracy Harmon had missed three deadlines, and the production and talent end of the company had sent him a brief memo saying that the boy had been missing dates for studio time and, when he did show up, was throwing tantrums. Furthermore, the little material he had turned in had been mediocre at best. With so much talent standing in line waiting for its chance, no one had time for this erratic behavior.

Jules's brief was to give the boy one final deadline and then they would cancel his contract. The word would be out that Star Records had dropped Tracy Harmon and the boy's career would be over.

How terrible, Jules thought, paying off the cab outside the Star Records offices at Rockefeller Center, to be a star at eighteen and forgotten at twenty. This was a rough world in the fast track, and not many had the stamina to survive it. Sometimes, Jules thought, it might be better if these youngsters didn't get the chance at all. For if they failed, they lived the rest of their lives with the knowledge that they might have been really famous, the biggest, and that was too much for them. They dropped away into drugs or booze or worse. . . . Jules's mind went back again to the headline in the newspaper. He never saw a headline about the industry without wondering who they had lost now. So many of even the very biggest, Joplin, Hendrix, the funny Mama Cass, even Dennis Wilson of the Beach Boys had taken another way out.

Damn that woman! he thought, riding up in the elevator to his twenty-seventh-floor office. All I wanted to do was read the headline.

What a city. New York had the best and the worst of them. Sometimes he wondered privately if the rudest people in the world came to New York, or if they got that way after they had lived there for a while. The green eyes faded back then into his memory, blazing with indignation, and he found to his surprise that his own anger wasn't gone. When he got back that night he might still go down the hall and teach that young woman some manners.

"Tallulah, get me a newspaper," Jules ordered, striding past his secretary into his own big corner office overlooking the ice rink. He shrugged out of his jacket and put it on the brass coat rack. Opening his briefcase, he took out the papers he needed for later and then stood looking down at the small rectangular indentation between the buildings where the ice rink was in the winter. The weather was still too warm for that, and the tables of the café that surrounded it were set out where the rink would be. Seen from the window, they looked like a flowerbed of blue and white daisies.

"Ho, ho, ho," Tallulah Golden said, coming into the office carrying a folded *New York Times* and a cup of coffee exactly the way Jules liked it, strong with a touch of cream. "Someone hasn't got fall fever."

"I'm sorry, Tallulah," Jules said, turning to face his longtime secretary. "Bad start."

Tallulah Golden came right out of the entertainment business, born and bred. At fifty, she carried more weight than her doctor thought good for her, but she carried it cheerfully and with the presence of a born entertainer. Her grandparents had both been vaudeville performers, and her father had been a Catskills comic who had never really hit it big nationally because his humor was "room humor," as they called it in the business. It went over in the small nightclubs but never could be tailored for radio or television. Tallulah herself had had a small success as a singer, but her type of singing, soft blues, had fallen in popularity. With a husband who had long ago disappeared and a son to support through college, she'd gone back to secretarial school.

But she still had the presence of a woman who might have been a star, and with her bright gold hair, she looked always ready for an appearance on stage. Her clothes still leaned toward the theatrical. That day, for example, she was wearing a vivid purple wrap-around dress above high spiked heels. She prided herself on her legs. Indeed, like many large women, she had remarkable legs, slim, finely shaped, real eye-catchers as she swung her full body down any avenue in New York. If Tallulah was alone, it was by choice. That was one of the many ways in which she and Jules understood each other. There were worse things in life than being alone if you knew how to handle it, and they had both learned that the hard way.

"Want to talk about it?" she asked.

Jules made a face as he sipped his coffee. "Some jackass girl down the hall," he said. "I think this city is attracting more and more lunatics," he said, opening the paper.

The headline he wanted read "Rock Star Declares for Senate." "Jesus," he said, pointing to the item. "You see this?"

Tallulah laughed. "Well, we've had an actor for president," she said. "What's wrong with a rock star for Senate?"

Jules just gave Tallulah a sour look.

"Hold that mood," she told him. "Today's meeting could be a lulu."

"How?" Jules asked.

"He missed another recording session." She put a memo on the desk. "The studio time with musicians cost ten thousand dollars."

Jules made no move to pick it up. "Get all the figures, will you, Tallulah," he said unhappily. "I better have them all."

"How you going to have them sit?" she asked as she started out.

Tallulah was a great believer in the theatrical. Once again, Jules agreed with her. The greater part of his office was taken up with his broad mahogany desk. There was also a couch, as well as two chairs and a coffee table, where he sometimes sat for the more relaxed meetings. For the tough ones Jules sat with his back to the window and the clients sat in straight-backed chairs upholstered in leather facing him. It made them understand who was boss.

"At the desk," Jules said. "No coffee."

"Got it," Tallulah said, and went out cheerfully. She had a vast compassion in her ample heart, but she was also realistic. She had been in the business too long to let every problem with the talent become personal.

Jules sat in his high-backed leather chair, put his papers aside and finished the small article on the rock star who was running for the Senate. As he read, his good humor returned to him. He was chuckling when he folded the paper again and put it on the corner of his desk. The star's platform seemed to be that everybody should hold hands once a day across the nation, and love would conquer all.

Tallulah had left his messages stacked in order of importance. He spent the next hour returning calls. He had almost forgotten the coming meeting when Tallulah buzzed him and he picked up his phone. "Tracy Harmon and his manager are here," she said.

"Give me five minutes," he told her. "Any other calls I should know about?"

"Nothing that won't wait," she assured him.

Jules cleared his desk of the yellow pad where he had made notes as he returned the calls, put the newspaper on the credenza behind his desk and placed the defaulted contract smack in the center of his blotter, where it would be the center of attention. He ran his eye down the figures that Tallulah had assembled for him, put them aside and stood up to put on his blazer.

Then he stood casually looking down at the café in the ice rink, letting the minutes tick by while the star and his manager cooled their heels outside his office.

Finally he pressed the buzzer on the intercom, sat down behind his desk and waited.

There was a discreet knock on the door and Tallulah opened it. She stood aside. "Tracy Harmon, Mr. Edwards," she announced in a businesslike voice.

Jules didn't rise.

A long-haired, blond boy-man came in. He was dressed in leather pants and cowboy boots, topped by a fringed suede jacket.

Jules let him swagger through the doorway without rising or smiling.

"And Mr. Harmon's agent," Tallulah announced.

Jules had been making eye contact with the boy, an old trick, unsmiling, firm, letting him know that this was a business office, not some club on the Sunset Strip.

Now he glanced over to the door, where the boy's manager would enter, and suddenly it was he who was off-balance. Striding through the door was a tall, slim girl with bright green eyes in an oval face framed by a mass of dark, tumbling curls.

Chapter Two

𝓕ifth Avenue was patched with the lights of offices, and in the narrow strip of night sky high above, the first stars glimmered as Jules walked home through the cool autumn night. He liked to walk in the city. He liked to feel the huge machinery of the metropolis changing gear from the frantic pace of the day to the high-energy pace of night. Sometimes he thought that there were two populations in New York, the day and the night, and that they worked in shifts. When the day shift was done those people went home, and slowly the night people came out to take over control of the city.

Beth had been a night person. She had

loved the night. Her career as a model had allowed her the great luxury of working her own hours, for she had reached that point in her career where she didn't have to accept every call. She was Beth Day, one of the city's best-paid models. When they had started out together, Jules was just out of law school, and Beth was a girl fresh from Iowa with a face that came along once in a generation, perfect, skin like the peaches that grew in her father's orchard, brilliant blue eyes and thick blond hair that hairdressers gasped over. They had gone out a lot. Beth liked Jules's connection with the entertainment industry. She liked to be seen in places and to meet people, "making contacts" as she put it. They went to all the right discos, and at Beth's urging, Jules wangled invitations to all the right openings and events, places where they would be seen.

Jules could still remember Beth's excitement the first time her name appeared in Liz Smith's column in the *Daily News*. "Beth Day, fabulous face for our times," the item had read, "and rising young entertainment lawyer Jules Edwards partied late into the night at Studio 54 along with other famous faces."

That item, cut out, had been taped to the refrigerator door in the old apartment, the first apartment that Jules and Beth had shared together way up Broadway in the unfashionable section. What Jules most remembered about that small apartment was that the counter in the bathroom was always clogged with Beth's cosmetics: to achieve that natural look took hours and hours.

Of course those famous faces had at that time no idea who Beth and Jules were. They were just two more faces in a crush of people.

As Beth became more famous and her face appeared on cover after cover and then suddenly one month as a two-story-tall billboard in Times Square, she herself became part of that glitzy, glamorous world that she had dreamed of in all those long quiet nights back in Iowa. And Jules was prospering too. His career had taken off like a rocket, for he had that rare blend of commercial instinct and artistic appreciation that made him the perfect entertainment lawyer.

They moved eventually from the small Broadway apartment. They were almost hysterical with happiness to be able to afford an apartment over the river with a view of the Statue of Liberty and another of the Empire State Building, which they could watch as they lay in bed together, dreaming of country houses and vacations. Jules liked to talk about children, too, for he knew he wanted children one day, but Beth was evasive. She had grown up in a farm family of six children, and she'd had to take on the chores of a mother too early in life to want to talk about children now. She wanted to talk about Milan, where the big fashion shows were held each year, and Paris and maybe one day becoming one of the super famous models.

The year they moved into the Riverside Drive apartment was the year the city started lighting the top of the Empire State Building with different colors on special holidays. Beth and Jules would lie in each other's arms and look at the New York skyline with the Empire State Building red and green and yellow on Columbus Day and think they were the luckiest people alive.

They bought an old car that year—an unheard-of luxury in the city—because they had a friend who lived at the boat basin at Seventy-Ninth Street. He had a free parking space that came with the slip for his houseboat. They drove the old station wagon out into the country every weekend and started collecting pieces of American country antiques. Small pieces at first—a chair, a table—and then as they got more money, larger, more important pieces—chests and rugs and finally their greatest triumph: an old dowel-posted bed. They had it all carted back to the city by a nice old Italian man from Brooklyn, who took almost as much pride as they did as they filled the big apartment with their prizes.

Life seemed nearly perfect. No, Jules corrected himself as he turned off Fifth Avenue toward the Plaza, perfect. He wondered why all this was on his mind that night. He hadn't thought of Beth in a long time. At first when she had gone he had thought of nothing else, but then finally her memory faded as his friends had assured him it would. He had been in such pain then that it seemed almost physical, but he knew now that he had held on to that pain long after he should have let it go because the pain was all that he had left of Beth, the pain and the loss. Once that was gone, she was gone too, forever, and that was a prospect he couldn't face.

The Plaza fountain was lit up, the water still running at this time of year. Soon the water would be shut off and the fountain would be dry for the winter, but tonight the water cascaded in brilliant silver light from the top basin and into the second, overflowing in a thousand strings into the wide bottom pool. Horses stood patiently by their carriages with their drivers, waiting for lovers to hire them for rides through the park.

The park was a froth of red and gold in the twilight, and Jules walked on into it, enjoying the warm night. He had trouble controlling his thoughts that night. Beth had been gone for five years, and he had learned to live with her loss. He had changed his life, sold the furniture and come to enjoy his solitude. He had bought the *Sapphire* two years ago, almost as a celebration after an incident that had shown him how much he had changed. Shopping for a light dinner one Sunday in Zabars, the big delicatessen, still dressed in the gray sweatsuit he liked to lounge around in on weekends, he had seen a fall of blond hair and had thought, I know her. For the smallest fraction of a second, the very tiniest fraction of time, he hadn't recognized her; then the recognition had come flooding in, and behind it, relief because he knew that finally he was free of his obsession. Friends had told him that she was back from Europe, but New York was a big city and he no longer moved in the night-life circles where he might have seen her.

The old-fashioned standard lights came on suddenly along the drive through the park. A horse carriage clipped by with its stands of paper flowers bobbing.

A lot of girls had come through his life since then. He didn't like one-night stands, but there had been a few of those also. He had gone back to sailing, an earlier, much more reliable and loyal love. He had had a couple of long affairs with girls he met out at the yacht club, sunny, outdoor girls with no chance of bringing up the mystery and power that Beth had held for him.

He had thought he was happy, unshakable, a whole man.

Until today.

He knew she had been as shocked as he had been when she had first stepped into his office, ready to do battle with this representation of corporate life. She had hesitated at the door and he could tell that she had been thrown off-balance by the sight of him sitting there behind the desk. She had put her hair up in a loose chignon, probably to make herself look tougher, but nothing could disguise the beauty of that perfectly oval face and the mouth that parted slightly in surprise.

She had been wearing a simple, unadorned gray suit for the occasion, but the jacket, loose and up-to-date, falling to her hips and held in a double-breasted fashion by one oversized black button, couldn't do much more to hide her fine figure than the champagne robe had done.

"You!" she said.

He found that, despite himself, he was smiling as he stood up. He fished in his pockets, and as she came uncertainly into the office, he leaned forward and put thirty cents on the desk. He saw the blood rise up the smooth column of her neck.

"For the newspaper," he said, making a joke of it.

She leaned forward and picked up the nickel. "You didn't take the whole paper," she said, smiling now too, though her cheeks were still rosy with embarrassment. "I think a nickel would be a fair price."

He held out his hand as he came around the desk. He could see from Tallulah's confused expression that he was breaking his own vow to be a hardheaded businessman. "Jules Edwards," he said.

"Danielle Martins," she said, and now she was laughing.

The boy-man rock star was leaning against the windowsill with his arms crossed, slouching sulkily. Jules looked him over and was about to offer his hand to him too, but the kid turned dismissively and looked out the window.

Jules's anger rose again and he was reminded of why they were there. He went back around his desk.

"Would you like a chair?" he offered Danielle Martins. She sat, crossing her perfect legs. He had a quick memory of how they had looked close up below the champagne silk. He pushed that memory from his mind and said to the kid singer, "Would you sit too, please?"

"I can hear you here, man," the kid said.

Tallulah watched with interest.

Jules said nothing for a long moment that drew out into an uncomfortable pause.

It was Danielle Martins who broke it. "Sit down, Tracy," she said gently.

The boy, for that was what Jules saw he really was, despite the fact that he must, if the records were right, be nearly twenty now, looked as though he might argue, but then he came over and sat down in the other chair facing Jules's desk.

Tallulah, in the doorway, cocked her head, made a big sign with one thumb and closed the door softly.

Jules looked at Danielle Martins. He found for a second he wasn't thinking about the contract. He was staring into the green eyes and thinking that he had never seen eyes that color. He didn't know that eyes came in that color.

She was watching him uncertainly.

He pushed out his own thoughts and looked down at the contract. "I guess you know what this is?" he said, looking from Danielle to Tracy Harmon.

Tracy Harmon sighed heavily. "Man," he said, "that's paper."

"Tracy," Danielle warned him before Jules could speak.

Tracy Harmon made a face and sighed as though the world didn't understand him. He might behave younger than his twenty years, Jules thought, but he was beginning to look older. The life of a rock singer could be a rough one. He had circles under his eyes and his cheeks were slightly sunken. Jules thought suddenly that the boy might be frightened. He probably knew how important this record was to his career. The poor kid, Jules thought. I'll bet he's terrified.

On that impulse he pressed the button under his desk and Tallulah appeared in seconds.

"Coffee?" he asked Danielle Martins.

Tallulah raised her eyebrows. This wasn't at all in the script for the meeting where Jules was to read the riot act.

"Yes, I'd love some," she said.

"Mr. Harmon?" Jules asked, stressing the "Mr."

The boy looked as though he would refuse

on principle. Then he said, "You got a Coke?"

"I think so," Jules said, and Tallulah went out.

There was a long silence then by mutual, unspoken consent. Jules could feel the tension drawing away from the room. He knew how terrible it could be to an artist to be blocked, unable to deliver a song or a book, finish a picture, all of it. And as the block continued, the fear would increase and feed back into the situation until the artist was paralyzed.

But he still had to deal with this as a business matter.

"We have to talk about this," he said to Danielle Martins and her star client, Tracy Harmon.

Tracy Harmon seemed to erupt from the chair. "Man," he shouted. "This is bull, you know. What am I, some type of butcher? You want me to make songs like sausages?"

He seemed to pivot on the worn-down heels of his cowboy boots. "Tell him!" he shouted at Danielle Martins.

Jules wanted to rise and grab the rude young pup by the neck and shake him hard. "Sit down!" he ordered in a voice that brooked no opposition.

The kid seemed to have been struck. His head went back slightly and his mouth flew open; then, as predictably as a kid, he shut it hard and his eyes narrowed as he prepared to protest angrily at this adult order.

But Danielle Martins was on her feet now. She placed both her hands on her client's shoulders and murmured soothingly to him as he let himself be led back to his chair. Jules found that he was watching the way she put her hand on the nape of the kid's neck and comforted him like a mother. He wanted to say, "Leave him alone. He's got to grow up sometime."

"Mr. Edwards," she said. "We need an extension on the contract."

Jules let the silence draw out again. He was in familiar territory here. He had a job to do, and he must do it.

"I don't know if we're talking about an extension, Miss Martins," he said evenly. He waited for her to correct him and insist she be called Ms. Some part of him even wanted her to ask him to call her by her first name, though he knew that would be unwise right then.

But he had made his point. He was threatening them that Star Records was about to cancel this contract. The boy made a small, choked animal sound, but Danielle Martins merely compressed her lips. She looked sideways quickly at the boy. She was strong, Jules noted. He had never come across her in the business before. That was unusual but not that unusual. She was young. Agents often combed clubs until they found one good "property," as they were called, then they dropped the rest.

Yet, Jules reflected as Danielle Martins prepared, by taking a deep breath, to answer his threat, she didn't have the toughness he was used to in artists' managers and agents. She looked vulnerable herself. When she blinked and looked at her hands folded in her lap, he thought for the briefest of seconds that the green eyes were moist.

He saw, however, that she was tough in a way he respected. Whatever her personal feelings here, she was dealing with the meeting professionally.

"Tracy is a very talented boy," she began.

"I'm not a boy," the kid said sullenly.

Neither Jules nor Danielle even looked at him.

"We know that, Miss Martins," Jules said. "Star Records has spent a small ransom fostering that talent. Now we have to be firm." He flicked the edge of the contract in a gesture he would have used on one of the bulletproof managers he was used to facing, and as he did so, he felt ashamed of himself. But if this girl was a manager of a rock artist, she knew as much about the world in which they both moved as he did.

This was real life, not some suburban, grass-covered playground. You got one shot at the brass ring before the carousel passed on and you gave up your colored horse to someone else.

"I'm sure he can deliver, Mr. Edwards," she said.

Jules could tell, however, by the pulse that was quickening in her smooth throat, that she was scared herself. He wanted to reach out and stroke her neck and say, "Don't worry. You're too good for this." For one terrible second he thought he might have spoken the words aloud, or even reached toward her.

He hated what he had to do. He took the small slip of paper that Tallulah had prepared for him earlier, and he moved it out from the corner of his blotter. Danielle Martins's eyes carefully followed the paper. Jules saw the boy was finally understanding the gravity of the situation, for he looked at the paper and then at Danielle with fear in his eyes.

Tallulah broke the moment by opening the door and coming in with a tray. For once, Jules was glad his finely prepared performance wasn't going to work completely. Tallulah bustled her cheerful way across the room and was about to put the tray on his desk when he said, "Over there

please, Tallulah," pointing to the coffee
table and the couch and chairs in the corner. If he'd asked Tallulah to strip down to
her underwear, she couldn't have looked
more surprised.

She took the tray over to the coffee table,
put it down and went out.

"Shall we?" Jules suggested.

The three of them got up simultaneously.
As Jules came around the desk, his hand,
sunburned and rough from his days sailing
the Long Island Sound, brushed Danielle
Martins. The fire that shot up his hand
might as well have been physical. He withdrew it fast, but not before he'd registered
the soft touch of her wrist. They stood
looking at each other, and then she blinked
once quickly and turned away, touching
her wrist with her other hand.

Anger rose again in Jules. He regretted
instantly that he had changed his plans for
the meeting. He felt confused and awkward, feelings that he hadn't had in a long
time. He picked up the piece of paper and
followed Tracy and Danielle toward the
sofa. "Look at this," he said roughly, thrusting the paper at Danielle as she and Tracy
sat.

She took it. Jules sat down in a chair,
trying to cover his anger. The boy looked
amused now. He seemed somehow to know

the worst was over and, like any spoiled child who has gotten his way once more, was prepared to flaunt his talent.

Jules picked up his coffee and ignored him.

Danielle Martins handed the paper wordlessly to Tracy Harmon. "What's this?" he said mock innocently.

Danielle sighed. "Tracy," she said, "this is the cost of the studio time for the sessions you missed."

Tracy Harmon shrugged. "What's money?" he said.

"Nothing if it's your own," Jules said roughly. "This is ours. We want it back."

The boy smirked.

Jules said to Danielle Martins, "We're prepared to extend for two more months. But we want double return on our money for the missed sessions, we want a bonus for the delay, and if he misses once more, we cancel, no discussion."

Danielle nodded slowly, looking at Jules with wide, wise eyes.

"Hey," Tracy Harmon protested. "He can't get away with that."

"Shut up, Tracy," Danielle Martins said quietly. "They can do whatever they want. It's their money."

Jules liked that. He had suspected she

was tough, and now he saw he had been right.

"Money!" Tracy spat again.

"I'm glad you feel that way," Jules said. "Because if you miss this one, kid, you won't have any. You're through."

Jules had the satisfaction then of seeing Tracy Harmon go white. He leaped to his feet and shouted, "Let's get out of here!"

Danielle Martins put down her untouched coffee, rose silently and held out her hand. "Mr. Edwards," she said. Her face had no expression, and yet still, Jules thought, she was perhaps . . . Even the thought tripped in his mind, and then it came rushing through. She was perhaps the most beautiful woman he had ever seen. Until this moment Beth had always held that prize, and he had accepted that she always would.

But Danielle Martins had pushed that image into the past.

Business, he reminded himself fiercely.

He shook her hand formally and then they were gone, leaving the door open behind them.

Tallulah appeared in the open door. She raised her eyebrows. "Two-month extension," Jules said.

Tallulah remained calm. She scrutinized

Jules with her big myopic eyes. "Good-looking woman," was her only comment.

Jules shrugged. "Beast of a boy," he said.

"Talent . . . ," Tallulah began.

"Get out of here, Tallulah," Jules said with a laugh.

She went, after clearing up the coffee cups and the Coke bottle, but Jules could tell that she was suspicious. Tallulah had lived a full life herself. She could smell attraction in the air the way others could catch the fragrance of summer flowers two miles at sea.

Now, as he walked out of the park high up on the West Side, Jules reminded himself that if he had one rule, it was that he never mixed business with pleasure. That way lay demons. He had seen it happen a hundred times in a business that was filled with beautiful women and handsome men.

The night air was cooler. There was the bite of winter in the breeze that came off the river as he turned onto Riverside Drive. All the windows along the drive were lit now, bright boxes in buildings that rose like cliffs to his left. He usually felt good at this point in his walk if he came home through the park. He'd had a good, hard day's work behind him, he'd had time for a round of squash at the club, and ahead of him was his apartment, where, when he walked through the door, he knew he was in his own private world, a place to recharge his batteries, as private as the *Sapphire* was in the summer when he took her with full sail out into the open sea.

Often in the evenings he'd have a date, but it had been a while since anybody special had come into his life. But he had learned to wait. You couldn't search. You had to just wait and be ready, make sure you were special enough yourself when that special lady came. He was seldom lonely these days. He knew that someone would come along eventually, and though he had stopped thinking about the house in the country or . . . or what? He chided himself, giving himself a piece of his own advice. Grow up, boy. This was real life.

Still, as he went through the doorway of his building into the inviting lobby, a trace of loneliness such as he hadn't had in a long time seemed to follow him like a veil of fog in a winter sea. He got his mail and went up in the elevator, flipping through the letters. Nothing but bills and leaflets.

The elevator opened and he was greeted by a long empty corridor; he almost had to laugh at himself for his feelings, for he knew what he was thinking: He was wondering if his neighbor's door would open.

Right now, he secretly knew he wouldn't mind being accused again of stealing something, her mail perhaps.

He laughed out loud at that. He was an overgrown schoolboy himself, a fool, he thought as he walked down the hall with his keys in his hand.

He saw the rose tied to his door handle at twenty feet, and his heart, whatever signals his panicked mind might start sending out, skipped a beat. The flower was yellow and seemed to draw him forward, glowing in the soft gray decor of the hallway. There was an envelope attached.

He untied the ribbon that held the flower and tore open the envelope. Inside was a month's subscription to the *New York Times* and a plain white notepaper on which was written in a strong handwriting, "Peace?"

The note was signed with a big *D*.

Chapter Three

*E*merald green eyes stared at him over the door chain.

"Hi," Jules said. His heart was beating like a teenager's. He knew he was breaking his first rule of business. The struggle had taken all of twenty minutes before he had said, "Oh, to hell with it," picked a bottle of wine out of the refrigerator and grabbed two glasses.

She was wearing reading glasses that were stuck into the thick curls on top of her head. "Hello." She smiled at him but she didn't make any move to remove the chain.

Jules held up the wine. "Peace offering."

The hesitation was clear. He had thought

the rose and the subscription were an invitation to friendship but now he wondered, and on the heels of that wonder came a gentle anger.

But then she closed the door almost all the way, removed the chain and held it open. She held her arms wide and said, "Sorry." He noticed that she was wearing an old gray sweatsuit with the legs climbing up the ankles and the top a size too big. "I was reading," she said.

"You look . . ." He searched for the word. "You look like a neighbor," he said.

She liked that. "Come on in," she said. "But I really do have to do some work. We're trying to find the right song to lead off the album and I've got pages and pages of lyrics to look through."

Jules saw that her apartment was much smaller than his, more a studio with a long deep living room and an L-shaped alcove where she had a high platform bed heaped in quilts. The living room was furnished with a deep couch in front of a tiny fireplace and two oversized cushioned chairs. All one wall was stereo equipment. On a long table that seemed to serve as her desk, hundreds of tape cassettes were lined up.

There was a nearly life-sized photo of Tracy Harmon on the other wall, which

Jules immediately recognized as the picture from the cover of Tracy's first album.

"I was always terrible at poetry," she said, crossing the room to put another small log on the fire burning in the grate. "And lyrics are poetry, aren't they?"

"I guess," Jules said. He liked this room. There was nothing pretentious about it. It spoke firmly of a woman who had made a home for herself around her own interests and needs. "I'm just a gunslinger in the record business," he said. "They bring me in to clean up the town."

Her glance slid toward the poster of Tracy Harmon and she smiled. "After I read through the songs, I have to play all those tapes," she said, gesturing toward the cassettes on her desk. "You wouldn't believe the awful material being written."

"Oh, I'd believe it," Jules said. He was beginning to feel foolish holding on to the bottle of wine and the glasses. He raised them up hopefully.

"Oh," she said as though she had forgotten why she had let him in. She had been watching him carefully, scrutinizing him almost. She went out of the room now.

Jules went over to the window. She had the opposite view from his, upriver past the marina toward the George Washington

Bridge. The bridge was two necklaces of lights strung against the dark night sky.

Danielle came back with a corkscrew. "I don't know how good this is," she said, handing it to him.

It was a supermarket corkscrew and Jules made a face at her. "Shame on you," he said.

She looked around the room as though she might apologize for it. "I'm not here much," she said. "I've been touring with Tracy almost all year, then . . ."

Again she looked at the poster, and Jules felt something else enter the room, something that he couldn't pinpoint, but he felt the anger coming back again. You're jealous, he told himself with amazement. He hadn't been jealous in three years, not since the awful rages that would course through him when he was out with Beth and other men made their interests clear. She hadn't exactly encouraged them, but then she hadn't exactly discouraged them either. She liked attention, any attention, and after the towering fights that she and Jules had had over her flirting, they had always fallen into bed and made love with a fierce passion that was part of the scenario, a passion that would leave both of them wet with perspiration, exhausted and drained.

For a long time, the making up had almost been worth the fights.

Jules struggled with the cheap corkscrew, and the cork finally popped with a loud gunshot in the room. It wasn't until then that he realized that there was no music playing. He looked at the stereo with his eyebrows raised. She was watching him warily from across the room, her arms crossed, and he almost wished he hadn't come. He had thought the note might be an invitation, but now he felt like an unwelcome intruder.

"You have to forgive me, Mr. Edwards," she said. "I listen to so much of it that sometimes I just long for quiet." She seemed to hear what she had said and she rushed on. "I don't mean that. I mean I don't want to listen to any more would-be songwriters croaking out their own lyrics."

While she was choosing music, Jules poured them wine. She came back as a soft fifties bluegrass song came on. Jules showed his surprise.

"Oh, I love country music," she said, taking the glass of wine out of his hand. "Good country music. I think that's about real life, don't you?"

He agreed. He could remember long ago on the drives in the country when he would tune in any country station he could find and Beth would hold her impatience just long enough to be polite before she changed the station.

"I mean it's about all the things that really matter, you know," Danielle Martin was saying. "Love and rejection and making up and loss. I can sit here and just cry my eyes out in a real orgy of self-pity on a night when I listen to good country music."

Jules laughed. "That would be a shame," he said. "Such lovely eyes, too," and he heard himself slide into the standard innuendo.

She cocked her head and stared frankly at him a moment before walking away to sit curled up near the fire.

The room seemed hot suddenly. The night was too warm, he thought. It was still too early in the season for the fire, and the wine after a long exhausting day must have hit him too quickly. Behind her he could see the night sky rimmed with the lights of the Jersey cliffs below and the stars above thrown carelessly across the black. The singer in the background was crooning a ballad of young love and early loss. Jules felt something rising in his chest that he hadn't felt in a long time, an ache such as he used to have when he had been a kid in

Maryland and he would go out on the small sailboat that his dad kept at the end of the dock. In those days Jules dreamed of what was ahead, where he would go, all the places he would see, people he would meet, and right at that point in the daydream a face, an image almost like a ghost, used to float somewhere in his mind just out of reach and he knew who it was. It was the girl he would one day meet who would make everything perfect. With her he would forget all the lonely times, all the work he had to do to get where he had to go. He found that he was smiling to himself.

"Why are you smiling?" she asked.

"I was just thinking of something that happened to me a long time ago."

She sat sipping her wine, watching him, and it came to him suddenly that she was afraid. "Listen," he said, "if you have work to do . . ."

Her mouth seemed to drop open slightly and her eyes widened. Again he thought the room must be too hot and the wine stronger than he had thought, for he had thought he had seen something more in her eyes, sorrow or fear, but it was gone before he could be sure.

She shook herself and put her hand into her hair to find the glasses that she had stuck up there. "Please . . . ," she said. "I'm being so rude." She stood up and came over to him and took the wine bottle out of his hand.

She poured more wine in his glass, and as she did so her hand brushed his and again he felt the touch of her skin through his whole body, an awareness of her that shook him. She stared at him for a moment before turning away to fetch her glass, which she had left on the hearth. As she did so, she casually turned on another light near the chair, changing the mood of the room instantly. The shadows fled and the walls seemed to move back. He guessed that she was trying to push away the feelings that he too had felt a moment ago when their hands met.

She turned with her glass, raised it and said cheerfully, "Neighbors."

He drank to that, but he wouldn't give in so much that he would repeat the toast. He needed a moment to think, to take a deep breath on his own, but he was afraid that if he left the room and went down the hall to his own apartment on some excuse, her ghosts would crowd into the room, again and that when he came back she would have some excuse not to see him.

Suddenly it was important—more than that, vital—to him that he get a chance to know this woman better. "Thank you for the subscription," he said.

She laughed. "Thank you for the extension on Tracy's contract," she replied.

Jules felt as though he'd just had cold water thrown on him. But he thought he knew what she was doing: She was protecting herself, reminding him that theirs was essentially a business relationship. When the first shock of the reminder passed, he liked her for that. "I hope he can do it," he said.

The shadow passed through the depths of her green eyes again and then was gone. "He will," she said with more feeling than he had heard in her voice. "He *has to!*"

"Strange business for you," he said.

"Why?" she asked.

"Well . . ."

"Not a good place for a lady?"

"Sort of," he admitted.

"Perhaps I'm not a lady," she suggested.

"Oh, you look like one to me," Jules said.

"That bad, huh?" she said.

"Listen," he said impulsively. "Have you eaten?"

She looked toward the door that lead to the kitchen. "I was going to fix something light," she said, and then looked at the table of tapes. "I have so much to do."

Jules drained the last of the wine into

both their glasses. "Come on," he said.
"There's a very small Italian restaurant
down the block. Do you know it?"

She shook her head slowly as she raised
her glass, then looked at him speculatively
over the rim. "I'm not here much," she said
when she had taken a sip. She looked out at
the river, where a tanker was moving like
some raffish dowager upstream, red and
green running lights glowing in the dark. "I
had hoped to be, but then . . ."

Again, the quick glance toward the poster
of Tracy Harmon. He was probably her
most important client, Jules thought. In
fact he was sure of it. The kid's problems
were therefore her problems. She must
have had some rough times in the last year.
He wanted to reach out and put his arms
about her and draw her to him and just
cradle her and say, "It's not worth it."

He had to take his bearings there for a
second, as when drifting off at the wheel of
the *Sapphire* when he was alone at the
tiller on a long haul. Sometimes when he
would come back, even a few seconds later,
he wasn't always sure if he had been gone a
minute or ten.

If she said no to dinner, he would walk
out. He would leave her politely and they
would indeed be neighbors. A part of him
almost wished for that. He knew what

would happen then: He would go down to his own apartment and open another bottle of wine, put on his own favorite music and have a light meal while he looked at the view. He would have a lot to think about because he hadn't felt this disoriented over a woman in . . .

But with a brisk shake of her head she said, "Fine. But a quick meal and then back to work."

"Great," he said.

"I have to change," she said.

"Me too," he said, looking down at the gray slacks that he was still wearing from the day. "But casual, very casual."

"Five minutes," she told him.

He handed her the empty wine bottle and he found that he was smiling foolishly. He felt light-headed from the heat and the wine. "Five minutes," he agreed, and he went toward the door.

"And Dutch," she called after him.

She was stating the ground rules. He turned and nodded gravely. "I could fight that," he said. "I could even pull the old expense-account routine, but all right, Dutch."

In the hall with the door shut behind him, he suddenly wanted to leap in the air for no reason. Well, tell the truth, he told himself, you know damn well why you want to leap in the air. But it was foolish. She had said "Dutch," and that made her own intentions as clear as she could make them.

As he opened the door to his own apartment, the feeling of excitement hadn't left. He stood for a second in front of the hall mirror, where Matha had followed his instructions of that morning and left a big arrangement of golden autumn mums. He made a face at himself, watching his self-satisfied grin. He raced into the bedroom throwing off his business clothes. He didn't need to search for what he wanted to wear. All his favorite old clothes seemed to come right to his hand: his faded jeans; his pale green flannel shirt that had once, a long, long time ago, been a deep jade green, almost the color of her eyes; his rain-stained cowboy boots.

When he was back in the hall he was facing another guy in the mirror. The businessman was back there somewhere among the clothes on the bedroom floor. This guy looked like a pentimento painting, the paintings that sometimes came out of old pictures when they were cleaned, earlier scenes that the artists had done and later overpainted. He looked younger, filled with an energy and excitement that he hadn't felt in a long time.

He was down the hall in a dozen brisk

strides, certain he would have to wait out there while she changed, but when he knocked, the door opened and she was there, ready, right inside.

He blinked in astonishment. "How did you do that?" he asked.

She was still the same woman, casual, her hair falling about her shoulders as though she had merely run a comb through it, but at the same time she could have gone anywhere, into the Plaza, to Regines, taken the Concorde to Europe. She was wearing pale fawn linen slacks over soft calf boots and a large darker leather jacket that fell loosely to her hips. Around her neck was a gold and green silk scarf that picked up the color of her eyes precisely.

He felt like a hick.

"Female wiles," she said with a broad wink, coming out into the hall. "That and a year on the road with a rock star." She locked her door behind her and looked him up and down. "My, my, my," she said, putting her arm loosely through his.

She had caught him off guard. It had been many years since a woman had done that. But he wouldn't go back and change. Damn her, he wouldn't. And somehow he knew she wouldn't have wanted him to.

They stepped out into the crisp, invigorating autumn evening. The wind blew in the

trees, tossing a few leaves lightly into the
air to fall and cascade ahead of them on the
street as they walked the half block, arm in
arm. Danielle held on to his arm, and he
felt unusually protective of the light touch
he felt there where her two hands rested.

"This is my favorite season," she said,
and looked quickly at him with her eyes
aglow. "I'm a sentimental softy."

"Not very good tools for the music business," he said. He felt both a kid again and
her older brother, her friend, a myriad of
persons, anything she wanted him to be.

"I don't know that I'm really in the business," she said.

"Tracy Harmon could be a very big star,"
Jules told her. "I call that the business."

They were at the restaurant now and the
conversation was dropped while they went
down the three brick steps and into the
warm lively interior. The tables seemed all
to be full with an argumentative but happy
New York dinner crowd, a local crowd who
gestured at each other with breadsticks and
leaned on the tables with their elbows. The
noise rose about Danielle and Jules like an
unexpected high tide, and his emotions
swelled with it. All the turbulence of years
before, when women were as mysterious as
uncharted seas, came back to him as
though he had never breasted the waves,

had never ridden the crest. He felt the uncertainty, the anxiety mixed with pleasure that he thought he had lost forever.

Danielle's eyes were sparkling at the sight of the crowd. "Why have I never been in here?" she asked him as though it were his fault.

"You need a passport," he told her gravely, "to get in here. We don't let just anybody in."

As if to prove his point, the maitre d' waved briskly from the back of the restaurant, and as they threaded their way through the tables they saw that a small empty table had somehow miraculously appeared in the corner. "Ah, Mr. Edwards," the maitre d' said. "Tonight if you order anything except the veal I shall cry."

"The veal is good?" Jules asked, then laughed as the maitre d' exchanged a look of masculine appreciation with him over Danielle's head as he held out a chair for her.

"Good?" the maitre d' said in mock horror. "This is a treasure. If I wasn't serving it to you, then I think it should be served only to the pope!"

Jules took his seat across from Danielle, who had opened the oversized leather jacket and loosened her scarf. He smiled to see that she still had on the sweatshirt underneath. She raised her eyebrows as she followed his glance. "My uniform," she said. "I'm afraid if I had my wish I would have sweatsuits in every color and wear nothing else."

Jules put his hand over hers on the table. She didn't say anything or take her hand away. They sat staring at each other and the friendship changed once again, quickly moving to some other place. The green eyes looked at him speculatively. She hadn't moved her hand, but he knew that in some way she had turned on another light the way she had up in her apartment. She wasn't moving away, but she was setting out her own boundaries too.

The maitre d' brought back a wine list.

"Wine?" Jules asked.

Now she took her hand away, moving it slowly from beneath his. He wanted to tighten his fingers and hold on to her, but he let her go.

"I love rough Chiantis," she admitted. "Is that being too much of a peasant?"

The maitre d' threw up his hands. "Peasant?" he cried. "Of course not! Wine is meant to be drunk, not stored forever in basements. You have the instincts of an Italian."

Jules raised his shoulders. "The house Chianti," he said.

"You have a fine woman here," the maitre d' told him seriously. "She knows value. She does not spend a man's money foolishly. Practical. This," he said, laying his hand for a second on her shoulder, "is a treasure, Mr. Edwards."

"You have a fan," Jules said. Then another, darker thought followed. "I suppose you have many," he couldn't help saying.

"No," she said simply. She knew what she was telling him. She looked at him directly. She had her hands folded simply in front of her, and she leaned forward, giving herself to his attention. "I've been too busy this whole year to do much but follow behind Tracy and pick up after him. He really is very talented, you know."

He sighed. "It's a trite observation, but you have to wonder if it's worth it, all these dreams they chase."

"We all have dreams," she said quietly, and he felt he had been corrected.

But that brought other thoughts too. What of her dreams? She couldn't be more than twenty-six or -seven at most. She looked a lot younger, but then most women did look younger than their age. She might, he thought with a kind of horror, be even younger, twenty-one or -two.

"How old are you?" he asked her directly, and she burst into laughter.

"The old right to the shoulder," she said when she had stopped laughing. Then, "I'm twenty-seven."

He had been right. He liked it that she was twenty-seven. She was a wonderful twenty-seven.

He had to remind himself abruptly amid all the cheerful noise of the restaurant that this was a dinner between new acquaintances, not even friends yet.

"And you?" she asked.

"Thirty-four."

He could see that she was assessing him again. The emerald eyes ran their glance over his face, stopping briefly at the small lines that were just beginning to appear at the corners of his eyes.

"I sail," he explained.

"They suit you," she said with a smile.

The wine arrived. She continued watching him while the maitre d' poured their two glasses of wine and left the carafe. He felt as warm and flushed under her gaze as if he had already had a glass of the full-bodied Chianti he now raised to her. She picked up her glass and they made a silent toast to each other.

"I think we should let Alfredo order for us," he said before the maitre d' could hand over the oversized menus.

"I agree."

"You are my favorite patrons," Alfredo said. "I promise you perfection."

They both laughed and Alfredo went off in the direction of the kitchen.

"A tough promise," Jules said. "Perfection."

Danielle tossed her hair back. "Are you a perfectionist?" she asked. "I think you are."

"No," Jules admitted. "But I think you should have some idea of what perfection is, even if you don't expect it. It keeps your standards high."

She sipped her wine, watching him again with those vivid eyes, and then she said, "I'll bet you're a nice man." The way she said it took Jules off-balance. There was little flirtatiousness about it. It was a statement of fact, or else a decision.

He laughed uncomfortably. "You seem surprised. In any case, I'm not sure I know what you mean."

"Decent," she said.

"Oh boy, you play unfair," he said. "That's setting standards right there."

"You were the one who said you believed in them," she countered.

"Touché," he said.

The room seemed to be warmer suddenly. In some way he seemed to be close to her already, very close, her eyes giving promises across the table from their depths, the little gold flecks that sparked at him were stars he could wish on.

But in other ways she seemed more mysterious now, further away, and he felt a sudden panic as though he had lost his balance and was slipping toward a rising, storm-tossed sea without a lifeline.

Everything in him wanted to trust her, to throw caution and his own rules away, but some far-off warning kept breaking through his dreamlike daze, a foghorn from a distant shore warning of shoals nearby, below the surface, that could wreck a man.

He tried to bring himself back to the present. "So," he said with decision. "Tell me, how did you come to be in this helter-skelter racket?"

She sat back and smiled a polite, first-dinner smile. "Oh," she said, "I drifted there."

"You don't look like a drifter," he said.

"You don't know me," she said. "I am. I was raised a drifter. Army brat. My father was a lieutenant general. We moved all over, Germany, Tokyo, Texas. I spent my favorite teenage years in Texas."

"The country music," he said.

"I guess."

Now he could detect the faintest of drawls, almost undetectable.

"I went to college in California . . ."

"Ah!" he said. "Bingo."

"Right," she said. "And I started out in public relations when I got out. I'm not a drifter maybe, but I'm restless. Always have been . . ."

"What company?" he asked.

She named a large talent agency.

"Pretty potent stuff," he said.

She smiled modestly. "I liked the business. I like talent, difficult as it is."

"You chose a tough business," he said.

She sighed and looked past Jules's shoulder to some place in her own memories. "It's not really a new story," she said when she came to the present moment. "My mother always wanted a career . . ."

"Singer?" Jules asked.

Danielle gave a small, sad smile. "Oh anything, more like it. She was a lonely woman. I don't know what she expected when she married my father . . . maybe to be a general's wife. It never happened, anyway. She just followed my father around from base to base, and he had his career and she . . ." She stopped. Jules could see her struggling with something.

When she started to speak again, he said, "You don't have to tell me this."

"No," she said, shaking her head slightly. "I haven't talked about any of this in a long time. She didn't have any talent, you see. She'd had dance lessons and singing lessons and all that. She'd been brought up in Alabama, good family and all, and she wasn't trained to do anything except amuse men. She had all these minor abilities but she always thought that if she'd been given a chance, she'd have been a star. She made us all miserable with her own unhappiness. She'd get drunk at parties and dance or sing, and if people didn't listen, she'd throw these awful drunken rages . . ."

"Like Tracy Harmon," Jules couldn't help remarking, almost to himself.

Danielle nodded slowly. "Except Tracy has talent."

"Yes," Jules allowed.

"Anyway, I decided pretty young that I was going to have a career. I saw what happened when my father finally had had enough. He didn't divorce her, because that would have been bad for his career. He just ignored her, and that was worse because she just sort of withered away in front of me. And one day . . ."

"Don't," Jules said.

"Well, you get the picture," Danielle said.

"Yes."

"It's not that unusual," Danielle said. "The worse part is that I had a sort of contempt for her when I was growing up. I saw her asking him for money for the smallest things, and I saw how she had to fool herself all the time, and I just swore it wouldn't happen to me."

"What about family?" Jules heard himself ask.

She didn't reply. She just looked at him and the question seemed to evaporate between them.

Alfredo shepherded a waiter toward them pushing a small cart on which sat a rough wooden salad bowl and an assortment of small dishes. "My own perfect Caesar salad," he said.

Jules picked up the carafe of wine and refilled his and Danielle's glasses while they sat back and watched Alfredo attend to his masterpiece. Alfredo smeared the bowl with a freshly cut garlic clove, picked up the bottle of oil, splashed it in and, spinning the bowl, added the other ingredients, the coddled egg (shells tossed aside quickly to the waiting waiter), the pepper, the lemon juice and the minced anchovies. The nearby tables watched, and he carried on a running commentary. At the last moment, in went the lettuce and the sprinkling of fresh Parmesan cheese. With a flurry it was done and presented to them as everybody nearby applauded.

Jules's mood was soaring as Alfredo served them the salad on chilled plates. At the first tart bite, Jules raised his free hand with his fingers clasped in the age-old gesture of appreciation. Alfredo shrugged in a small, falsely modest gesture of his own that made everybody laugh and applaud again.

Alfredo withdrew and Jules looked at Danielle as she ate with gusto.

"What are you thinking?" she asked suspiciously.

"I was thinking," he said, "that I wouldn't want to be anywhere in the world except right here."

Time missed a beat before she said quietly, "Yes."

They didn't need to talk after that. They finished their salad and the veal came. It was as perfect as the salad, and with it was a pasta dish that was both creamy and light. Jules felt lighthearted and giddy. Every so often he had to look across the table at Danielle Martins to make sure that she was really there. Every time she caught him, she smiled mischievously. Once he caught her looking at him the same way.

"Caught you," he said, and was rewarded by seeing a blush come to her cheeks.

She put down her napkin and touched his hand where it lay on the table. "You don't know how much I'm enjoying this evening," she said. "Lately . . ."

He had seen Tracy Harmon in his office. He had an idea of what her life had been like lately. He turned his hand over and took hers in his. Her skin was soft and smooth and he could feel the touch of her right up his arm and through his whole body, a drug coursing through his veins. He squeezed her hand more firmly and she left it there for a second more before taking it back.

"I'm not getting much work done," she said bemusedly.

Neither of them wanted dessert, but they both wanted a strong espresso coffee.

"And a Sambuca," Jules said.

"Oh, no," Danielle protested. "I really have to get to work!"

He looked at her and she shook her head in exasperation. "All right," she said. "I feel like some irresponsible schoolgirl. I'll probably choose some terrible songs for Tracy to listen to tomorrow and he'll think I'm off the tracks too."

The waiter brought them espresso and tiny glasses of clear liquor with three coffee beans floating in each.

"We haven't talked much about you," Danielle said.

He didn't want to. He didn't want to have to talk about any of the past. He wanted to talk about . . . He caught himself. She was right. She had work to do tonight and he was a lawyer. This was a business relationship. Oh well, maybe more, a neighborly dinner and perhaps later, one day, they would become friends, but this was a dinner to make up for a misunderstanding, nothing more.

He felt his good mood draining away. "I am what I seem," he said.

"Are you?" she asked. "Not many people are."

"I'm an attorney," he said. "As you know. I grew up in Maryland. My father was a doctor; my mother stayed at home and was *extremely* social. They both loved me a lot. They sent me to a fine prep school when I was fourteen, and later to Princeton for my undergraduate degree. They encouraged me to go to Harvard for my law degree and paid for that too. They were fine people, and I owe them more than I can ever repay."

"Were?" she asked.

He nodded, the dark cloud moving closer. "Car accident," he said. "Slippery road. Christmas."

He'd never talked about that, not even to Beth. It had happened, a clap of thunder and part of his life had changed irrevocably. Even now his heart seized up and he could feel some, though not all, the feelings that he had had that night when the call came: the shock, the anger, and later, for months after, the regrets that he had never expressed his own feelings of love and gratitude toward them. There had always seemed to be so much time. He had never imagined that they wouldn't be there for him. They were that type of family, privileged but normal. Things like that didn't happen to them.

Mercifully, the check came to stem the dark memories and to stop the conversation. He felt as though he had said too much already—had betrayed a part of himself he didn't want to share.

Danielle took out her credit card.

"Please?" he said, and he made it a plea.

"Dutch," she insisted. "We agreed."

So they divided up the check, making a joke of it. When Alfredo came by and saw what they were doing, he cried, "Mr. Edwards. A treasure! A treasure! A woman who pays for her own dinner." He seemed as shocked as he was admiring.

Jules had feared he might lose a few points in Alfredo's eyes—a man who would let a woman pay for her share of the check —but Danielle had become a mystery to Alfredo, a beautiful woman with a complexion like a Naples dawn and eyes like the depths of a Sardinian sea, and one who would pay her own way. It shook Alfredo so much that he hurried away and came back shortly with a small nosegay of tiny pink carnations, which he presented to Danielle.

She put them in her collar and thanked him. As they stood to leave, she whispered to Jules, "I don't think Alfredo thinks I'm feminine enough. He's encouraging me to take lessons."

They came out into a night as black as sables flicked with silver. Jules put his arm about Danielle's shoulder as she pulled her jacket closer. She looked up quickly at him, and her face was so near he could have kissed her by merely leaning forward. "I've had a wonderful night," she said.

"Me, too," he said. It wasn't enough, but it was simple and she understood.

The awkwardness came as they went into the lobby, where the doorman bowed to them, and again as they rose up in the elevator. On their floor, he walked her to the door, where she got out her keys with a trembling hand. She wouldn't look at him as she fumbled with the lock, but finally he took the key from her. She kept her gaze averted as he slid the key into the lock and in one strong movement pushed open the door.

When she turned and opened her mouth to say good night, Jules placed his lips on hers in a kiss as hot as a glowing ingot. She gasped, and he felt her hands come up to press him away, but the fire passed through her as strongly as through him, and she fell against him. They took each other hungrily, their mouths locked and time fleeing away from them. Then Jules did what he had never even imagined he would do. He picked her up and took her into the dark apartment, closed the door behind him with his heel and placed her very gently on her bed.

Their mouths found each other's again and their passion flamed up as they explored each other first gently and then more fiercely with their hands. Their clothes seemed to drop away, and then he saw her naked. He couldn't suppress his own shock: She was beautiful; he had expected that, but not this beautiful. Wide sculpted shoulders bracketed firm, well-rounded breasts; a slim smooth waist flared to full padded hips leading to a voluptuous curve of thigh and calf so beautifully outlined against the sheets that he now ran his hands down them, uncertain before so much perfection.

But she helped him, reaching up with her arms and pulling his strong body against hers. They caressed each other, her white flesh pale under his dark, sunburned body. When they could stand it no longer, he felt her shift beneath him slightly and he raised himself and, taking her to him, began to take his last knowledge from her. She cried out in pleasure and then they were together, moving on a tide of passion that rose and fell. He could hear her soft cries as they became one, and then time lost its meaning as the sea took them, drowning them in pleasure so intense that it was close to pain.

They dropped away gradually into sleep, their bodies intertwined. Jules was soon lost in a dream of the *Sapphire* thrusting forward on a sunlit sea toward a distant, barely seen shore, a line of pale sand against a cloudless blue sky. Nearby he knew there was someone whom he loved as he had never loved before, though as he sat at the helm guiding the sailboat he couldn't see her, only knew she was there, trusted, loved, treasured.

He woke once in the night to find Danielle curled up with her arms about his neck and again he was amazed by her perfection. He cradled her as she murmured in her sleep the little cries that had awakened him. Adjusting the blankets over them, he whispered words of love and she quieted again in his arms. When he closed his eyes, he let his happiness take him back to where he had been when her cries had first awakened him.

Chapter Four

$\mathcal{N}$either of them knew what to say when they awoke. Danielle opened her eyes feeling the warmth and comfort of Jules's arms. Her face lay on his chest, which rose and fell evenly as he slept.

In one night his body had become as familiar to her as her own. She breathed the fresh musk of his skin and felt that she could close her eyes and lie there safe for a long, long time.

Jules opened his eyes. He knew Danielle was awake though she had closed her eyes quickly when his breathing hesitated. Her hair, below his chin, was as fresh with lavender as the night before, and her skin where he held her was as soft as violets in the spring.

He thought, What have I done? He had violated all his own rules. He had mixed business with his private life.

But then she stirred and his body began to respond to her, their skin touching along the length of their legs and thighs. Her breasts moved against his chest and his arms tightened around her, drawing her closer still.

Her eyes opened, staring up at his with their green depths. He could see fear there. She was waiting for his decision. He knew what he should do. He should get out of bed, allowing the awkwardness that would grow between them to restore their distance.

Instead he tilted her head and, leaning down, placed his open mouth on hers, exploring her again with his lips and his tongue. He felt her whole body relax in his arms as she gave herself again to him, meeting his unspoken questions, the questions of his mouth, with her body. He ran his tongue down the line of her ear, tracing it onto her throat, and she arched with a whimper of pleasure. He was at the delta where her throat met her chest, exploring between her breasts. He licked the crevice where they met while his hands played with her nipples, the rough skin of his sailor's palms caressing the satin swelling of her breasts.

"Please," she murmured against her will. "Please, Jules."

But he moved his hands, letting them slide lower while his mouth followed where they had been, taking each nipple in turn in his mouth, circling it with his tongue until he felt it rise, nibbling gently while his hands cupped her buttocks, pulling her closer. Her hands took the hair at the nape of his neck, pulling on it gently, then harder as she arched beneath him, pushing his head further. He was at her most secret place and he raised her to his mouth, pulling on her teasingly with his teeth, probing with his tongue, licking until she opened and then deeper, deeper while above him she cried out and her legs locked in pleasure around his neck.

"Jules!" she cried.

He came to her, crushing her with his body as he moved up to take her lips with his again, and then she was bucking slightly, her head back as she clawed at his back with her fists. He entered her strongly in one thrust, and the cry erupted in her throat and she lost her breath. He withdrew and plunged again as she rose to meet him. Her breath expelled near his ear in pleasure and then they were one again as they had been the night before, locked in a rhythm that took both of them higher and higher, beyond themselves, rising to a moment when both of them clutched at each other desperately, calling to each other from some lost place.

Afterward they held on to each other, damp skins together, until their breathing was even again.

Danielle slipped out of bed, taking the top sheet with her. Wrapping it around her, she went into the bathroom and closed the door behind her.

Jules lay naked on the bed. He had made love to two dozen women, more, since Beth had gone, and to each he had thought he had made love, but his night with Danielle had brought back in a rush what he had been missing, what he had lost: the feel of two people who needed each other and shared a passion that overwhelmed them in every part of their bodies.

Danielle opened the door. She had run a comb through her hair and splashed her face with cold water. She looked as beautiful as a woman who had spent hours in preparation. The lovemaking had left a flush on her skin, like the first blush of a young girl, and as she came toward the bed she was smiling.

She sat down beside him and he placed his hand on her wrist.

Neither of them spoke, but their eyes explored the depths in each other's, looking for secrets, answers, commitments.

Satisfied, Danielle leaned down and placed her head against his chest again, and he held her for a few minutes, feeling such an overflowing gratitude that he thought his eyes might have watered as they did in a high wind as the *Sapphire* plunged through a high sea.

He loved her.

The thought came as clear as the cry of a gull.

She felt his arms tighten around her and she looked up questioningly.

He couldn't bring himself to tell her that. Instead he looked at her, hoping she could read the expression in his eyes.

She moved away and, grinning, he tightened his grip.

"Oh no, sir," she said, reading his intention. She tried to pull herself from his grip, but he held her to him with arms made strong from hauling on the rigging in fifty-knot winds. She struggled briefly before collapsing against him.

He kissed her lightly, unable to say the words that filled his heart.

Instead he said, "I make a fine breakfast."

He saw the thought that passed through
her eyes, a dimming of the luster in the
green depths. She thought he had spoken
those words to other women, lots of them,
and made them breakfast too.

And he had, the exact words, but not as
he spoke them today. He had spoken them
as a ritual they all understood, all the
adults of the city, but now he was saying
them to Danielle because he couldn't bear
the thought of leaving her for a minute.

"I don't want to leave you," he said quietly, coming as close as he could to all the
feelings that moved within him. "Come
along to my apartment." And then, realiz-
ing it like some gift thrown their way by a
beneficent deity, "It's Saturday."

She blinked, and then by the way her own
smile grew, starting slightly at the corners
of her lips and spreading into a wide mis-
chievous grin, he knew that her own pleasure matched his.

She sat up. "All right," she said. She
couldn't take her eyes off him. "You go
ahead. I have to shower."

"I'll wait," he said.

She laughed. "I won't be long."

"I'm not letting you out of my sight," he
told her.

She examined his face a few seconds more before getting off the bed. She tried to take the sheet with her again, but he took the corner in his fingers until it caught and pulled away from her. She was naked in the sunlit room before him. Her body was a flawless landscape of swelling curves and smooth planes, and by the way she stood straight and unashamed, he knew that she was proud of it. She smiled at him before walking across the room and into the bathroom.

Jules put his hands behind his head, grinning broadly, very satisfied with himself.

Through the window he could see light clouds moving majestically across a clear blue sky. On an impulse he picked up the telephone by the bed and called the garage where he kept his car and told them to bring it down. He felt buoyant, happy, filled with an energy that he hadn't known he had missed. Warning thoughts, dark clouds on the blue horizon of his day, kept trying to break through his contentment but he pushed them firmly away.

Danielle came out of the bathroom rosy from her shower. She was toweling her hair.

"Come over here," he said.

"Oh, no," she said. "You keep away from me, you brute."

"Then all I can do is get up, I guess," he said.

"You got it."

Jules got up and pulled on his old jeans. It had been years since he had felt so much like a college boy, tumbling out of a strange bed with a beautiful girl and his old familiar clothes on the floor. These days his seductions were all . . . all well planned, he concluded, pulling on his flannel shirt. Either the girl or he knew exactly what was to happen, both of them generally, and by mutual consent. Often with the agreement unspoken, they moved from one stage of the evening to the next, even setting alarm clocks if one of them had to work early.

The sex was good and necessary, but not like with Danielle the night before when both of them had been taken by something greater than themselves.

"What are you grinning at?" Danielle asked suspiciously.

"Male things," he said, teasing her.

She stood holding the towel in her hand and looked at him. Somewhere in the night her own suspicions had disappeared. He could see the trust in her face. His eyes wandered to the cleavage of the toweling bathrobe where the soft swell of her breasts were.

"Quick," he said. "Dress. I have a surprise for you after breakfast."

"Oh, Jules . . . ," she said, looking at the tapes on the desk. "I have to work."

He sat on the couch. "Then I'll just stay here," he said.

She stared at him.

"Go on," he said. "Work."

He could see the struggle within her. "What's the surprise?" she asked.

"Oh, no," he said. "You must give yourself to me today. I'll lead."

She dropped the towel on the floor and came over to him and sat on his lap. She didn't say anything, but the look in her eyes as her face moved close to his was filled with a happiness that mirrored his own. She kissed him lightly on the lips and then laid her head on his shoulder. She smelled of lavender and talcum powder. He could feel his body stirring at the nearness of her.

She did, too, and got up, but not before she had hugged him tight. If she had given him some extraordinary gift, his own feelings at her arms around him couldn't have been more . . . he searched for the word . . . more grateful. While she fumbled in her closet for some clothes, he had to look away to make sure he didn't make a fool of himself by blurting out too much.

He had a feeling that he had escaped some near disaster that he hadn't even known was nearby, as though the *Sapphire,* sailing on a clear open sea, had been about to strike a hidden reef unmarked on any map.

He knew what the disaster was, too; he was smart enough for that. He had been about to walk, with his eyes open but blind, into that desert of the heart where people met, coupled and parted, thinking they had everything—jobs, friends, homes, all the things that to the outside world seemed so important but actually were as nothing to the one quality that made life worth living: true feeling. He had seen it happen to so many of his friends, men and women who became so self-sufficient that they thought they needed no one else, and then after a while, almost unnoticed, the light seemed to fade from their eyes as though, like pearls left too long in a safety-deposit box, they were slowly dying from within.

Danielle said, "Jeans or a skirt?"

"Jeans," he told her.

She dressed quickly in neatly pressed jeans and a beautiful oversized navy blue sweater. She shoved her feet into soft pigskin shoes, grabbed up a satchel that matched, and tied a blue and gold silk scarf around her head. "Okay?" she asked.

"Perfect."

They went down the hall to his apartment, and as he let them in, Jules said, "No one escapes this place without pulling their weight. I run this like a ship. You get to make the coffee while I change."

But Danielle stood transfixed just inside the door. "This is beautiful," she said, looking at the vast expanse of his living room with the leather couches, the fireplace, the walls of books and stereo equipment and the broad view downriver all the way to the Statue of Liberty. She watched a cruise ship moving slowly up the river, pushed by two anxious little tugs, while a sailboat made her cautious way toward the harbor mouth.

Jules put his arm around her and stood beside her while she took it all in. When she looked back at him finally, he thought he saw some change in her eyes. It made him uneasy.

"It's only an apartment." He apologized as though somehow he had overwhelmed her with his success or money or career, the way men in singles bars gave their credits right behind their name. "Hi, I'm Joe; I'm a lawyer; I drive a Porsche."

She didn't respond, but he could see that something else had entered their relationship, some element that hadn't been there a moment before. He was used to that when women saw the apartment. Sometimes he saw calculation, and sometimes just simple reassurance in the insecure ones: they wanted to be with a successful man, and here, all about them, was evidence that they had chosen right.

But he had a sense that that wasn't true of Danielle. She seemed almost uneasy as she went in the direction of the kitchen.

In the shower, he ran the water as hot as he could stand it and scrubbed himself down roughly before passing to his bedroom to choose a fresh flannel shirt faded to the exact right color of pale blue. He buttoned it over his favorite jeans and pulled on his cowboy boots. The face in the mirror wouldn't stop grinning at him.

"You idiot," he told it. "You really think you're something, don't you? Well, you better watch your step with this lady. She's special."

So warned, he went back out to find Danielle sitting on the window ledge with a cup of steaming coffee, looking down at the river. He came up beside her and ran his hand under the full fall of dark curls at her neck. She looked up at him and he kissed her lightly on the lips.

She smiled at him but she was lost in her own thoughts.

"Breakfast?" he asked.

"Famished."

She followed him into his kitchen, where every device that Macy's had ever carried seemed to be displayed in the proper place. She poured him coffee while he took eggs and green peppers, scallions and cheese out of the refrigerator. The coffee when he sipped it was exactly right—strong, nothing weak or apologetic about it. She stood and watched him while he grated the cheese for the omelettes and cut up the peppers and scallions. She didn't offer to help the way other women did, and he liked that.

He popped the English muffins in the toaster, handed her a knife and turned his attention to the stove. When the butter had melted to the right smoothness in the copper omelette pan, he seemed to throw everything together with one twist of the wrist and seconds later there it was, the perfect omelette.

"Bravo," Danielle applauded.

When he had done the second omelette, he led her back out to the raised dining area in a corner of the living room. They sat across from each other and he lifted his freshly filled coffee cup to her. "To our meeting," he said.

She smiled and returned his toast. "I'm glad we met, Jules," she said. Relief flooded through him. He knew that she had made some private decision of her own and that he had been accepted.

She ate heartily. When breakfast was over she said, "Now you sit there, and I'll get more coffee and clean up." She put her hand on his shoulder and gently pushed him back into his seat. She took the plates away and he could hear her rinsing them and placing them in the dishwasher. When she came back with the coffee pot, she poured more coffee for both of them and then sat across from him, crossed her hands under her chin and looked at him mischievously. "You're trouble, aren't you?" she said.

"I don't think so," he said slowly.

"Oh, I think so," she corrected him. "Big trouble. But I'm a big girl and I guess I've been warned."

They stared at each other across the table, taking a new measure. They both liked what they saw.

"I suppose I should say I don't do this all the time," she said. He could see that she knew she didn't have to tell him anything of the sort.

"Well, I'm glad you made an exception," he teased, and she burst out laughing.

Then suddenly she stopped laughing and she drew a deep breath.

"What's wrong?" he asked.

She didn't reply right away. When she did, she first said "Nothing," then immediately corrected herself. "You'll think I'm an awful fool for telling you this," she said, "but I thought for one second there I was going to cry." She looked at him with fear.

He had had a similar moment and he might have told her that, but he couldn't. Instead he reached out with his hand and took hers. "I don't think you're a fool," he said.

The tears weren't entirely banished. She had to blink. "It's been such a long time since I've felt this good," she said.

"Me, too," Jules said simply, and he held on to her hand until he saw that she was in control again. .

Now she laughed at herself ruefully. "Boy," she said. "You're lethal, Jules. I'm afraid to ask why you're still walking around free."

The dark clouds that had threatened earlier and then vanished loomed again on the horizon. Danielle caught the change in his mood right away. She turned her hand to take his reassuringly. "Don't," she said.

But by the way Danielle held his rough hand in her soft one and looked at him down the table, he had a fair idea she knew that there had been a disaster in the past.

"Let's begin right here," he suggested.

"No past?" she asked.

"Just you and me."

"Okay," she said quietly.

She took away the rest of their dishes and then Jules said, "You'll need a light jacket."

"Will you trust me to go get it by myself?"

He took both her hands in his. "You promise not to vanish?" he asked.

"I promise."

"All right, but just for a minute."

She left, and Jules was alone in his apartment. He stood in the center of the living room listening to the silence. It was as though he hadn't seen the room before. A bachelor's apartment, he thought. A confirmed bachelor's apartment. The apartment of a man who likes to be alone and intends to stay that way for a long time.

He walked to the window and looked down at the small marina across the street. He felt uneasy. He had met a girl who brought back all the best feelings he had ever felt about love, but he had become used to his life. Like a dark shadow, the ghosts rose up now and began to mock him. He had felt this way before, and then . . .

But Danielle was back with a light knock on the door. He opened it and took her into his arms, pressing his lips to hers in a hunger that was meant to banish the past as he had promised—as they had promised each other—and at first she was surprised. Then her own passion met his and they kissed each other with the fire that they had felt the night before.

When they stood back Danielle said, "You do like surprises, don't you?"

"No," he said, opening the hall closet and taking out his own weather-beaten windbreaker.

She looked at the notation "Sapphire—Southampton—St. Thomas" on the pocket.

"You'll love her," he said. "She's the most beautiful sailboat in the Western Hemisphere."

They went down in the elevator arm in arm, and the doorman gave them an expression so lacking in anything that he might as well have winked.

Danielle laughed. "Thank God my mother can't see this," she said. "She'd be all ready to take you straight to city hall for a license."

The day was a full Indian summer with the sun high in the sky and the leaves on the trees bright gold and red and bronze in the still air.

When they got to the garage, the car was waiting. Danielle breathed a sigh of relief.

"What's that about?" he asked her.

She pointed to the beaten-up maroon station wagon in which he hauled the gear for the *Sapphire*. "A nice sensible car," she said, as he opened the door for her.

Jules loved to drive. The moment he sat behind the wheel, all his troubles always seemed to flee. There were times when, driving out of the city, he wondered why he worked so hard, why he spent so much time dealing with spoiled talent and crazed business managers when what he really wanted to do was take the *Sapphire* down into the islands and start a small charter boat operation. He would dream of that as he drove out along the Long Island Expressway, imagining what it would be like to wake up every morning with a blue sea below the black hull of the *Sapphire,* a golden sun, arching palm trees over pale pink beaches and nothing to worry about except finding a school of barracuda for his guests. His own needs, despite what his apartment and his life in general might show, were simple. He had never wanted great sums of money. He had planned his future with Beth: a house in the country, days of small delights, nights of whispered secrets. They had been like two conspirators: They told each other their dreams, and if those dreams in the early days included high times among the jet set, it seemed, at least to Jules, that they were visitors there.

They had come to the city like the country mice, not really expecting to be taken in by all the glamour. They had thought of themselves as outsiders who would peek at the way the rich lived, and then go home together to giggle under the sheets, holding tight to each other as they reaffirmed their own, simpler dreams.

But it hadn't happened that way. The other life had taken Beth, seduced her like a siren song, and then she was gone and he was alone.

He found his own pleasures, more solitary ones than Beth's, but rich none the less, luxurious, filled with a self-indulgent comfort that had required hard work and money.

Sensing his mood, Danielle reached over and placed her hand on his knee. His ghosts vanished, fleeing in disarray into the past. "Where are we going?" she asked.

"My secret," he said.

"I'll bet you have a lot of them," she said, and though she tried to keep her tone light, she couldn't meet his eyes.

She was a strange girl, he thought. She had secrets of her own that he hoped one day she would give to him in trust.

He drove across the Triborough Bridge, weaving quickly through all the traffic and then out onto the parkway. The city dropped behind them, and soon they were in the country with the hills rolling away in every direction, flowing with the gold and red colors of autumn. Jules turned off the parkway, choosing instead the smaller back roads.

Following a train of thought of his own, he asked, "Do you think Harmon will deliver?"

She started as though he had fired a gun inside the car. Jules looked at her quickly. She was fumbling for her satchel, which she had dropped on the floor. "Yes, of course!" she said.

She fished a small handkerchief out of her satchel but didn't seem to know what to do with it.

"Are you close to him?" Jules asked.

The green eyes glanced sideways at him and for the first time he thought he saw suspicion there. "Why?" she asked.

"Look," Jules said, "I'm only asking a question."

She relaxed, but the small handkerchief was balled tight in her hand. "No," she said, looking out the window.

Jules didn't press her. In the distance a picture-book farm appeared on the crest of the hill: a rambling white house, a red barn, a tall silver silo and, making it all one, a graph of roughhewn log fences. Two horses cantered across a meadow, tossing their heads in delight at the warmth of the late-fall day.

"He's . . ." She watched as the horses wheeled and came back across the meadow, kicking up tufts of the soft ground. "He's had troubles and he's really a very sweet boy. "He's . . ." She tried to find the word she wanted. "He's good," she said, looking at Jules.

"And scared?" Jules asked.

"Yes," she said.

He knew exactly what the trouble would be: the first record would throw a boy like Tracy from a simple life, where music meant everything to him, into a whirlwind. Where before he would have worked hard on his music and been his own worst critic, suddenly people would be saying that he could do no wrong. Jules could imagine what the youngster had gone through surrounded by flatterers who would push him further and further to the outer limits with their praise, offering him easy sex, drugs, anything that they thought would make him take them along for the ride. They would bleed him dry, and then when the carnival stopped, they'd drop him cold while they went on to leech off the next fresh success. He'd seen it a hundred times and the script never changed, but the youngsters coming up always thought that they were different, they would beat the odds.

There were exceptions, of course, but not many. And some of course did beat the odds; some took a long, cold look at what was happening around them and cleared all the parasites out of their lives. But the waste of human lives in the music business, the waste of the freshest, youngest, was its tragedy.

Jules slowed the car as they came to the crest of the hill, and below them was a small country inn with a brook running beside it. He had been there often. When he'd asked Danielle to trust him today he hadn't had any exact destination in mind. He loved driving. He loved getting out of the city. He had never entirely gotten used to city life, though to an outsider, he supposed, he was the epitome of city life. But deep inside he was still the boy who had grown up in a warm family with a nice house and a backyard that rolled away into the Maryland countryside.

On any summer day he would have taken her to the *Sapphire,* but the *Sapphire* was on her way south. And now suddenly he was confronted with the Seven Cedars Inn, where he and Beth had come so often.

At the sight of the small inn crouched

below the tall cedars, Jules's heart contracted. He wanted to drive past but Danielle cried out, "Oh, how beautiful!"

Jules made his decision. The ghosts could do what they wished. He turned into the yard.

Mrs. Samuels, who owned the inn, must have recognized the battered station wagon, for she came out as soon as they pulled up, drying her hands on her apron. She was large, comfortable and red faced, everything an innkeeper should be. She beamed at Jules.

"Jules!" she cried, and then, seeing Danielle get out the other side of the car, she stopped. Her smile widened in a slow delight.

Then it hit Jules. He had never brought any other girl here. He had come here with Beth, and after Beth was gone, he had come here alone often, usually in the fall and winter, sometimes to stay overnight and sometimes just to sit by the large fire and listen to the brook outside the window. But he had never brought a woman here since Beth.

The mind was a strange thing, he thought as he went forward to hug Mrs. Samuels. His mind had made this decision at some deep level without his ever thinking about it.

Mrs. Samuels hugged him back hard before going forward to greet Danielle.

"This is Danielle Martins," Jules introduced her.

Mrs. Samuels made no bones about looking Danielle over. "My, my, my," she said.

"And this is Mrs. Samuels," Jules said.

"Call me Flora, dear," Mrs. Samuels said. Jules could have been knocked into the creek by a gust of wind.

He showed Danielle his surprise with a look over Mrs. Samuels's head, and Danielle understood instantly. Laughing, she allowed herself to be borne away by Mrs. Samuels toward the inn.

Jules followed the two women into the low-ceilinged building. The legend was that George Washington had spent a night there, but as Mrs. Samuels said, "If George Washington slept in every inn in New England that claimed he did, that man couldn't have won the Revolutionary War!" The Seven Cedars Inn had been in Mrs. Samuels's family for six generations. The great sadness in her life had been to have her only child, a son, killed in Vietnam. Now the inn would one day have to go to strangers. "But not until I'm dead and buried myself," she had said defiantly.

Jules did all Mrs. Samuels's legal business free of charge. He loved the bustling, warm woman, and though she had never said so, he knew she loved him too. They had shared their own grief together without ever saying a word.

The dining room had two tables filled with city dwellers out for a country drive. Flora Samuels took Danielle and Jules through to the smaller dining room, which she kept open in the winter. From there she could supervise the staff with her wise New England eyes and still have Jules and Danielle to herself.

She sat them down at a table that overlooked the brook where the trees crowded the banks. The water, spotted with falling leaves, swelled past the window.

Flora Samuels sat down herself. The sigh of satisfaction she gave as she looked from Jules to Danielle made him burst out laughing. "Mrs. Samuels," he cautioned her.

"What have I said?" she asked innocently, spreading two plump red hands wide. "Now, dear," she said, ignoring Jules and turning to Danielle, "tell me all about yourself."

Danielle blushed very nicely and Jules could see that Mrs. Samuels approved of that. Mrs. Samuels had strong opinions that most of the time she kept to herself. She had liked Beth, but as Beth became more and more high-fashion in her dress and more peremptory in her manner, Mrs. Samuels's silences had spoken more than words ever could.

Danielle said, "Well, I was born in Texas. My father was an army officer. I went to school at the University of Southern California and now I work in the music business."

None of that told Mrs. Samuels what she really wanted to know. She focused her clear gray eyes on Danielle.

"She's single," Jules said, smiling at Mrs. Samuels.

Mrs. Samuels sighed.

"You old devil," he said. "You couldn't bring yourself to ask straight out, could you?"

"He's a wicked boy," Mrs. Samuels told Danielle, her eyes bright with happiness.

"I'm beginning to discover that," Danielle said, looking at Jules.

"But he's a fine man," Mrs. Samuels hurried to add. "A good man."

An echo of Danielle's comment that Tracy Harmon was "good" came to Jules, but he had other things he wanted to talk to Mrs. Samuels about. "I was hoping," he said, "we could get you to make us a picnic."

"Oh, my," Mrs. Samuels said, clapping

her hands together. "There's a nice roast chicken just waiting for you in the refrigerator. And there are the last of the tomatoes just off the vine."

Jules kissed Mrs. Samuels on the ear. "You spoil me."

"Someone should," Mrs. Samuels said with a heavy emphasis, looking at Danielle. "A man needs to be spoiled or he turns."

"Turns?" Jules asked. "You make me sound like a milk carton left in the sun."

"You know very well what I mean, Jules," the old woman said.

"It seems to me," Danielle said, "that he spoils himself."

Mrs. Samuels drew a deep breath into her ample bosom. "That's just modern living," Mrs. Samuels said, and it wasn't hard to understand what she thought of modern living. "All that going to fancy restaurants and meeting loose . . ."

She stopped. Danielle had passed some mysterious test of Mrs. Samuels's and she was now in the category where "loose women," which was what Mrs. Samuels had been about to say, couldn't be mentioned in her hearing. Jules wondered how Mrs. Samuels knew about "loose women." He'd never brought any of them here. This was his sanctuary, as the *Sapphire* was.

Mrs. Samuels went off to the kitchen and Danielle rested her head on Jules's shoulder. It was a moment or two before he realized that she was laughing. He was chagrined.

When she stopped shaking with laughter, Danielle said, "Oh Jules, forgive me, I'm not laughing at you. It's just that you looked so caught there when Flora was talking about"—Danielle raised her eyebrows—"loose women," she whispered.

Jules could feel the flush of embarrassment rising up his neck.

"Please," Danielle said. "Smile. You've got to admit it's funny."

He allowed her a small smile.

But now her laughter had faded and she was looking at him seriously with her beautiful eyes. "I hope you realize," she said, "what a lucky man you are."

"Today I do," he said.

The way she looked at him, he knew she felt the same way. Nothing else needed to be said, and they sat holding hands, watching the leaves float past on the surface of the bubbling stream.

Mrs. Samuels came back with the picnic basket covered with a red and white checkered cloth. "It's so nice to see people who are happy." She smiled. "I see so many who come here who aren't."

She shepherded them out through the big kitchen, where the staff were working. Mrs. Samuels did most of the cooking herself in the winter, but in the summer she needed help for the heavy trade. The inn was at its best in winter, and Jules had a fleeting happy thought of coming here with Danielle later in the year when the snow would lie upon the land for as far as they could see, blue white in the moonlight, and the silence would be like the silence in a cathedral.

Danielle and Jules walked off, he swinging the basket with one hand while holding hers with the other. Danielle slipped her hand out of his and took his arm tightly, resting her head against his shoulder as they walked.

"Don't say anything," she said. "Please. I can't believe this is happening."

He led her through the lower meadow and then into the dark stand of woods at the other side. Here the sunlight pierced the branches of the trees to dapple a carpet of leaves. The only sound for a long time was the shuffle of their feet in the fallen leaves. A rabbit stood up ahead of them, both white paws dangling in front of him, a look of such outrage on his face that both Danielle and Jules burst out laughing.

The woods thinned and the shadows

faded and they were out again in clear land near the top of the hill. Jules led Danielle along a path that seemed sunk in the earth. "The Indians came this way to hunt the animals that would drink from the stream in the winter," he told her.

"We haven't improved on the quality of life much, have we?" Danielle said.

"No," Jules said. "We just made it more complicated."

"Do you ever wish you'd lived in some other time, some simpler time?" she asked.

"No," he said, considering her question. "I used to want another life," he said. "A simpler one."

She didn't ask what had happened to that dream, and they came now to the place he had wanted her to see. He had discovered it himself on one of the long solitary walks he had taken the first year he had been alone.

The land fell away at their feet to a natural delta in the curve of the hill. Here Jules had sat hour after hour watching the vast landscape that stretched away to the distant horizon. Not a house was in sight. Everything was as it must have appeared to the first settlers, virgin land of natural meadows and thick forest veined by the silver river.

Danielle dropped his arm. She stood looking down the slope of the hill. Her eyes took in the rich green flanks of the meadows, the burning golds of the turning leaves, and the river that reflected the round disk of the sun spreading its blessing over the autumn landscape.

"You don't play fair, Jules," she said.

"Not when I want something badly," he said.

She looked back at the land. He put down the picnic basket and took her in his arms. "Are you cold?" he asked.

"Superstitious," she said, looking into his face so close to hers.

He kissed her, his mouth taking her lips in his as he held her against him.

She pulled away, and then came back to him again and lifted her face to be kissed once more.

"Okay, buddy," she said briskly when he released her again. "Food. None of this love stuff."

Jules made a move to grab her, but she nimbly evaded him and picked up the picnic basket. She lifted the cloth to show a plump chicken roasted to a crisp turn, home-grown tomatoes, a loaf of fresh-baked bread, and two ripe peaches. Mrs. Samuels had put in a big bottle of her own homemade cider.

"Well, that decides it," Danielle said, looking at the feast. "I'm not going back. I'm staying here forever."

She laid out the cloth and started to put the food out for them. Suddenly she laughed. "Oh no, that old devil." She held up a cigar.

"Mrs. Samuels," said Jules, "has her own ideas of what's right for a man."

"Like a woman to wait on him?" Danielle teased.

"Sounds good to me," Jules said.

"Ho, ho, ho," Danielle replied. "The true colors show."

They sat out of the wind in the lee of the hill and ate lunch. The sun was warm on their faces, and afterward Danielle leaned back against Jules and together they looked down the valley at the peaceful landscape. Jules thought he had never been so happy. At some point he fell asleep with Danielle cradled in his arms, and when he awoke he was surprised to see that two hours had passed. Danielle's head was against his shoulder and the palm of her hand on his chest. Her long dark eyelashes fluttered as her eyes followed some dream of her own, and again, as the night before, she cried out gently in her sleep, a cry of pain that made Jules tighten his hold on her.

Her eyes opened quickly. He could see

that for one second she wasn't sure of where she was.

"It's all right," Jules whispered to her. "I'm here."

She looked at him with wide open eyes from which the fear had not entirely vanished. He wondered what it was that could so frighten this beautiful woman that her dreams were haunted, but he knew he couldn't ask, not yet. He wanted more than anything to take care of her, to keep her safe, to send those dreams of her sleep fleeing and bring back to her the happiness that she deserved.

He watched the fear vanish from her eyes as they met his. Leaning down, he whispered, "I love you, Danielle."

Chapter Five

The silver jet shot skyward, engines screaming. Jules was pressed back in his seat. The last two weeks had been the happiest he had had in four years, and even now, as he left on a business trip for California, he felt as though he were moving in a dreamworld.

Tallulah had been properly skeptical. She had known Jules through the troubles with Beth and after that, through an assortment of other women. She had learned which calls to put through, which to take information from and which to shield him from. But he had walked right into the office the weekend after he and Danielle had gone to the Seven Cedars and said, "If Danielle Martins calls, put her through wherever I am."

"Wherever?" Tallulah asked, with both thin, plucked eyebrows rising.

"Yes."

Tallulah followed his progress on into his office with a look that he knew meant the third degree. He had broken his own cardinal rule not to mix pleasure with business, and Tallulah wasn't going to let him off easily.

He shucked off his jacket, opened his briefcase and spread the papers out on his desk. He was dialing the telephone when Tallulah arrived with his coffee. He tried to show her that it was a personal call by waving his hand, but Tallulah could avoid a signal better than a New York waiter when she wanted.

"Hello," said Danielle on the other end of the line. He could picture her in her apartment at the desk of tapes she had to listen to.

"Hi, it's me," he said.

She laughed. "Hi, you," she said.

"I just wanted to know if you missed me yet," he said.

Tallulah spun her good-sized body as though on a dime and looked at him with openmouthed shock.

"You just left twenty minutes ago," Danielle said.

"It seems longer," Jules said.

"Go to work, young man," Danielle told him. "I have to."

"Okay. Okay," he said. "But you'll see. You'll miss me later and have to call."

"I miss you already, but I have more character than that," she said. "I love you. Go to work."

"Me, too," he said, trying to avoid saying the words in front of Tallulah, who had developed an intense interest in the ficus tree by his window.

Tallulah turned as he hung up.

"Not one word," he warned her.

"Have I said anything?" she asked innocently. And then, "Good weekend?"

"Out," Jules ordered her.

"Boy," she said in mock chagrin. "I get to hear about all the bad times, but when the good stuff happens, it's 'Out.'"

She went, letting the door say everything she couldn't say about how she felt. Jules knew she was joking. They had helped each other through more than one rough moment and were as much friends as boss and secretary.

He sat back in his chair, looking at the view of downtown New York, the Empire State Building, the Chrysler Building and, all the way at the end of the island, the World Trade Towers. He sighed with satisfaction. The world seemed a fine place to be.

He took the time to savor the memory of the weekend before the telephones started to ring and his day became totally crazy. They had sat on the hillside until the sun sank in the west, spilling a gold cloth across the valley, and the sky shaded to a pale gray that quickly became night. The wind had risen, creeping round their shelter until Danielle had shivered and Jules had thrown all the remainders of the picnic into the basket.

They made their way down the hill in the darkness. A small sickle moon appeared in the black dome of the sky, and then, as sharp as diamonds, stars.

Danielle pressed closer to Jules as they passed through the dark woods. They breathed in the smell of the fresh fallen leaves underfoot as they walked on toward the far sparkling light that was the inn.

Danielle whispered, "I feel like Hansel and Gretel."

"If Mrs. Samuels heard that she would pop you in the oven," Jules said.

Danielle giggled. "You know what I mean."

Mrs. Samuels was in the kitchen when

they arrived. The inviting smell of a roast leg of lamb tantalized their nostrils. "There you are!" Mrs. Samuels said. "I was going to send out the dogs to search for you."

Jules said in embarrassment, "We fell asleep."

"The lunch was delicious," said Danielle.

"Wait until you have dinner," Mrs. Samuels said with pride.

"Oh, we can't stay, Mrs. Samuels," Jules said.

Mrs. Samuels put down the basting spoon she was holding. "Not stay?" she demanded. "And why not, may I ask?"

"We have to get back to the city," Jules said.

"And what's there?" the plump little woman asked in indignation, "that you can't have here better?"

Jules looked helplessly at Danielle, who said to Mrs. Samuels, "We'd love to stay."

"There you are then," Mrs. Samuels said to Jules as though he were still putting up objections. "I've already had the girls put fresh sheets on in the Valley Forge Room. You go right on up there and freshen yourselves for dinner."

Jules and Danielle went out obediently. He knew where the room was, though he had never stayed in it. The Valley Forge

Room was the best room in the house, the room Mrs. Samuels kept for honeymooners, and there weren't many of those coming to this quaint little inn. Most honeymooners went to the Caribbean or California or south to Florida these days. He knew the door would be unlocked. That was another of Mrs. Samuels's quirks. She refused to allow locks and keys to the doors. There were latches on the inside the way there had been a hundred years ago.

He led Danielle down the uneven hall scattered with rag rugs done by the Samuels family, and under the low arch that led down to the original wing of the inn. He opened the door to the Valley Forge Room. An old brass kerosene lamp glowed softly on the mantel and the four-poster bed was turned down with crisp cotton sheets. From somewhere Mrs. Samuels had found a pair of men's pajamas and a nightgown. They lay ready on the counterpane.

Danielle giggled looking at the pajamas. "Mrs. Samuels isn't quite up-to-date," she said.

"You bawd," Jules told her. "Respectable women still wear nightgowns, I hear."

He closed the door behind them and took her in his arms. "I should have carried you over the threshold."

The kiss seemed to go on for a long, long time, and when they broke apart, both were breathless.

Danielle said, "I feel I'm on some sort of roller coaster and there's no one at the controls." She shivered.

"I'm here," he said. He realized as he said it that he knew almost nothing about her: he knew all the superficial facts, but he knew nothing about any other lovers, any disappointments or heartbreaks. The roller coaster had moved fast for both of them. Yet they had made their pact not to talk about the past, to start fresh.

"Dinner won't be for a while," he suggested softly in her ear.

He lifted her up and carried her to the bed. She clung to him like a child, and when he laid her down on the bed she still kept her arms about his neck, drawing him down toward her. Their lips met again like old friends and they held on to each other gently as their desire increased. First Jules slowly undressed Danielle with shaking hands. He took his own clothes off roughly and came to her where she waited for him on top of the coverlet. Her arms closed about his back, her hands clutching him as he entered her. She arched against him with the cry of a lost doe. He took her for his own pleasure while her fingers tore into him, until his need was satiated and a cry of release burst from his throat.

For a long moment she said nothing, then, as they pulled apart, she rolled aside, turning her back on him and he felt her shaking with sobs. He put his hands on her shoulder but she didn't respond. "I'm sorry. Oh, darling, I'm so sorry," he whispered.

She cried silently with her back turned to him. He felt in despair at his own selfishness, afraid that he had lost her. He had found her and now he had lost her.

But he said nothing, merely held her, and finally as the tears subsided, she turned without looking at him, and he knew by the way she circled into him that she forgave him.

They slept. A light knocking at the door woke both of them at the same moment. Jules shouted, "One moment."

He jumped from the bed and moved across the dark room to the door, but he only opened it a crack. A smiling maid stood outside. "Mrs. Samuels says that dinner is about to be put on the table." Jules could see that she was about to giggle. He had a good idea what they thought in the kitchen of his and Danielle's arrival.

"We'll be right down," he said.

He closed the door and went back to the bed.

"Beast," said Danielle, and then she giggled. "It's not fair," she said. "Women should be able to rape men."

He was forgiven. He kissed her lightly. "Anytime," he whispered in the dark.

"You may be surprised," she said to him as he sat beside her on the bed.

"Well," he said, "if you need any practice, I'll be glad to teach you." He almost leaped out of the way before her foot reached him, but not quite, and he rolled off the bed onto the floor with a thump that he knew they could hear in the kitchen below.

"Beast," she repeated.

Jules stood and turned on the low table lamp by the bed, then got back in beside her, and they lay wide-eyed, staring at the low ceiling with the axe marks on the age-bowed beams. Jules turned his head for a kiss, and afterward his eyes roamed over the small fireplace in which Mrs. Samuels had arranged for an unlit fire to be waiting for them.

"We forget, don't we, how good living can be." She had caught his thoughts drifting.

"We make our choices," Jules said.

"Yes," she agreed, and there was a sadness in her voice to match his. Again he thought she was an unlikely girl for the business she was in.

They dressed and went down to the dining room. A waitress showed them to a quiet table that Mrs. Samuels had clearly chosen for them away from the other guests. A bottle of red wine stood open, breathing to come to full bouquet.

"How she spoils you," Danielle murmured.

"It's not always like this," Jules told her. "I've slept in the attic room when the inn was full and been pressed into service as a porter if she needed extra hands."

The waitress arrived with a salad of watercress picked by the brook. The sharp pepper taste prepared their taste buds for the rest of the meal.

Jules poured the wine. He said, holding up his glass, "I don't know what to toast."

"Today," Danielle said.

"The future," he suggested. "Today seems so . . ."

But before he could find the word he needed she said, "Today," and he saw that the sadness was back in her emerald eyes. He didn't press her.

Mrs. Samuels arrived pushing the cart with the roast leg of lamb, which was crisp on the outside but the most perfect pink in the center. She handed Jules the carving knife. "I like a man to carve, don't you, dear?" she said to Danielle.

Danielle snuck a quick look of conspiracy at Jules, but it didn't go unnoticed.

"Oh, I know what you're thinking," Mrs. Samuels said, unperturbed, as Jules stood over the leg of lamb and began to carve expertly. He could remember Sunday dinners at home with his father carving and the same warm feeling of family about him. "You're thinking," Mrs. Samuels said, "of all those women's rights that I see on the television when I have time to look at it—the devil's box as it is, with all that terrible trouble brought right into your own home. But I say it's fitting for a man to do certain things and a woman others, which doesn't mean a woman can't do most of the things a man can do. I run the inn now that I'm alone, and if I say so myself I do a good job; but it's not like it used to be when I ran part of the house and my dear husband the other. I never felt oppressed like I'm told I was meant to, but then I'm a simple woman."

Neither Jules nor Danielle was about to accept that evaluation of Mrs. Samuels, and they let her know it by their laughter.

"Well," she said with satisfaction,

spreading the apron she still wore, "it's good to have a man here."

"Please join us, Mrs. Samuels," Danielle said.

"Flora," the friendly woman corrected Danielle.

"Please, Flora."

"No, no dear," Flora Samuels said. "There's a time when two people should be alone."

Jules served the roast and the perfect parslied potatoes and fresh carrots.

Danielle said, "I feel as though all I've done for twenty-four hours is eat and make love."

"Sounds fine to me. I'll sign on for a longer tour of duty," Jules said.

The kick he got under the table made him swear aloud, and the waitress, who had been hovering in the doorway, put her hand over her mouth to suppress her giggles.

"We're a public scandal," Jules said.

"Ummm," Danielle said, enjoying the meal.

Afterward they went up to their bedroom, taking with them a small silver tray with an authentic silver coffee pot from the time of the Revolutionary War, and two fragile porcelain cups that Mrs. Samuels's great-uncle had brought back from China when he was in the opium trade. Jules lit the fire. They sat contentedly without speaking while they had their coffee until it was time to go to bed.

Once in bed, they lay watching the fire, which filled the room with a golden glow.

Danielle lay with her head on Jules's chest. The smell of her body was now as familiar to him as his own, and their limbs seemed to rest comfortably entwined without any awkward shifting.

"Marry me," Jules said suddenly.

"What?" Danielle looked shocked.

"Marry me," Jules repeated.

"Oh please, Jules," she said, "don't do this."

"Why not?" he said.

"Everything is so perfect," she said.

"It could be this way forever."

She didn't reply to him right away, but her face was inches from his and he knew with a sadness that came into his own heart like a morning chill that she would refuse. "Do you think it would ever work?" she asked, and he knew she was asking him a real question.

"Yes," he said, praying that something would change in a moment, that some Pan, god of the woods, who looked after lovers, would enter the room unnoticed and change the words he knew she would say.

"I don't," she said flatly. It was almost a confession and more, an acknowledgment of some deep hurt of her own.

"Let's take what we have and be grateful," she said.

He was silent a long time, still holding her. From the feel of her quickened heartbeat against his naked chest, he knew she was afraid that he would say something hurtful and spoil their time together.

"I love you," he said finally.

"You don't know me," she whispered into the mat of hair on his chest.

"I know all I need to know," he insisted.

They were drawing apart, they both felt it. Jules bitterly regretted that he had rushed her so fast, but he had felt so right, so perfect with her, that the words had seemed to come out of his mouth of their own volition. Then they began to make small movements with their hands and bodies together, to come back to each other. Soon they were making love again, almost fearfully at first, then with more joy, and finally as one person, as they had the night before. When they finally fell off to sleep, the words that had frightened Danielle and almost spoiled their time together seemed to be forgotten.

In the morning they drove back into the city in a contented daze and spent the day and night in Jules's apartment working quietly on their own work. Jules sat at his desk and examined the briefs that he had brought home from the office, making notations on long legal pads. Danielle sat with a small tape recorder on her lap and earphones around her head, listening to tape after tape while she made notes of her own for Tracy Harmon's recording session, which would be coming up while Jules was in Los Angeles.

He hadn't brought up again his wish to marry her, but he hadn't changed his mind either. That night she had insisted on going back to her own apartment and he hadn't pressed her. Still, when he woke in the middle of the night, his heart raced in a panic he hadn't felt in a long time. He knew exactly when his heart had last raced like that. It was when Beth had gone and it seemed as though part of him had been cut off.

He lay awake once he was calm, watching the dawn gray the sky over the river through the window. He had found someone precious. He had thought that once before and had lost her. He was determined it wouldn't happen again.

Tallulah, of course, had her own views. She was bursting to tell him, and over the next two weeks he let her drop hints like the leaves that fell from the trees, but he wouldn't give her so much as the slightest opening.

Finally she marched right in at the end of the day and said, "This is for your own good."

Jules cocked an eyebrow at her. "Every time someone has said that to me it's been unpleasant," he remarked.

"This is after hours."

She was right. They had been buddies and he had cut her out, but he didn't want to share anything of what he and Danielle had exchanged for the last weeks.

"Okay, Tallulah," he said, "get your coat. Let's hit Arthur's for a drink."

"Good boy," she said.

Danielle was off with Tracy Harmon doing rough tapes of the songs she had chosen. He would record fifty songs over four days of intense work; then they would cut that down to twelve and later mix in the orchestra with electronic mixing behind him. The record would cost over a hundred thousand dollars to record, before even one disk was pressed.

Danielle was nervous and skittish, and she had asked if Jules would mind if, when she got home later that night, she went straight to her own apartment. He did, of course. Well, one part of him wanted every moment of her time, but the other admired her professionalism. He had never seen a business manager who took such close interest in her client. Every moment of her day over the last two weeks had been spent with Tracy Harmon, hand-holding him through the first rehearsals.

"You're good," Jules had tried to tell her gently when she lay in his arms at night. "You can manage other singers, you know, if he can't make it."

But she had taken no solace in his words, and he had seen a faint shadow under her eyes as the recording dates drew nearer.

Tallulah appeared in the doorway with her raccoon coat on and fresh makeup. "Better to be looked over than overlooked," she said merrily.

Jules grabbed up his own navy cashmere overcoat and they went down in the elevator. Outside the night was cold with the first strong breath of winter blowing down the avenue. People hurried home with the looks of small animals heading for their burrows.

Tallulah took Jules's arm and they walked toward the West Side until they came to Arthur's. The bar was four deep with men and women from the advertising and fashion industries, but Tallulah managed to push their way through to a table in the corner.

"I hope you know what you're doing," were her opening words when Jules's scotch and soda and her martini had arrived.

Jules sighed. He was going to be given a lecture.

"She's wonderful," he tried to explain.

"She's business," Tallulah said.

"No," Jules said. "You don't understand, Tallulah, she's different."

"Jules," Tallulah said—after hours they were on a first-name basis—"if you knew how many times I've heard men say that in this business."

Jules could feel himself getting angry. He wasn't sure if it was the stifling heat of the bar, or the small, cramped space, or just that in their pleasure in each other he and Danielle had seemed to get little sleep in the last weeks, but he could feel his control slipping.

Tallulah saw the flush that had come to his face. "Look," she said, "you're talking to a veteran of the war between the sexes, Jules. I've broken every rule in the book and I have the scars to show it. Let me tell you, they don't call these rules clichés for nothing. They're clichés because they happen so often."

"But not always."

Tallulah took a good healthy belt of her drink. "Not always," she allowed, but Jules could see he hadn't convinced her.

"Tallulah," he said, "please, I think I know what I'm doing. She's a wonderful girl."

Tallulah sighed. "I just don't want you hurt," she said.

He knew what she meant. She meant she didn't want him hurt the way he had been before.

"I love her, Tallulah," he said.

The wise eyes blinked and she looked at her drink. "Have you told her?" she asked.

"I asked her to marry me," he said.

"And?"

He couldn't bring himself to say the words that Danielle had spoken when she refused him.

"I see," his friend said.

"But I'm going to keep right in there trying," he said.

The way Tallulah pursed her mouth told him more than words would.

"Keep your fingers crossed, Tallulah," he asked her. "Please?"

She nodded and tried to muster a smile, but he could see that he hadn't banished her worry, only increased it.

"I have to go," he said. "Can I walk you to the subway?"

"No," she said. "I think I'll stay for a little while."

He stood up, leaned over and kissed her on the cheek. "Don't be such a pessimist," he said with a smile. "Magic still happens. You've just been around the record business too long."

"I hope you're right," she said before he turned to go to the bar to pay the check.

Jules was thinking about his conversation with Tallulah as the plane leveled out and banked to turn away from the glittering city below. Below him the lights sparkled like jewels all up and down Manhattan Island, and the rivers ran dark as black gold. Jules sat back in his seat feeling the good sort of loss, the loss of going away for a short time to work at his craft. Danielle was down there, and while he was away for ten days, she too would be working—in the recording studio with Tracy Harmon. When they next met, they would meet with the hunger and anticipation of a separation that would have taught them how much they needed each other.

Jules thought of a line he had read somewhere. "It is a good thing to miss someone before they are gone." He missed Danielle already, and he hoped she would miss him as much, because when he came back he intended to press his suit again.

He would prove cynical Tallulah wrong. Magic did happen. There, shining in all its glory far below as the jet bore him away toward the sun of the other coast, was the magic city. Miracles had to happen, for that was what kept men believing.

Chapter Six

$\mathcal{H}$ i."

"Hi."

"What are you doing?"

"Well, I was about to go to sleep." Danielle's voice was filled with the suppressed laughter that Jules loved.

"I wish I were there," he teased.

"Well, I'm very pleased you're not," she said across the long-distance line. "If you hadn't gone to California, I would have had to run away myself to get anything done. How are things out there?"

"Relentlessly cheerful," Jules said. Through the window of the bungalow he had just checked into at the Beverly Hills Hotel, he had a view of arching palms and the thirties elegance of the four-story pink main building. A blond woman of such perfect beauty that she seemed more assembled than real was walking along the path lined with bushes flaming with garish orange bird-of-paradise flowers. A small dark man with gray hair was talking rapidly to her as though cueing her.

"I miss you," Jules said. As he said it, his heart missed a beat, then raced ahead driven by some unknown fear of its own.

"Darling, you've only been gone six hours," Danielle said.

"I hate it," Jules said. "Let's never be apart again."

The long pause before she replied made Jules's heart start its race again. "Is anything wrong?" he asked.

Danielle's voice, when she replied, had a sadness in it. "No," she said.

"Something's wrong," Jules insisted.

"No," Danielle replied quickly. "Nothing's wrong, Jules. Everything's perfect. Maybe that's the problem. I don't believe things can be this perfect, do you?"

"No," he admitted. He ached to get on the plane and fly back to comfort her.

"I love you," she said. Jules could still hear the sadness in her voice.

"Believe," he said.

"What?"

"Believe," he told her. "Some people must find perfect love. Maybe we've been lucky."

Then he heard tears, though she quickly put her hand over the receiver so he wouldn't know she was crying.

"I'm coming back," he said.

She gave a long sniff into the telephone. "No, please, Jules, don't. It's just that I miss you too, so much. I can't believe I'm acting like this. I was going to be so cheerful and here I am crying."

"You're sure everything's all right?" Jules asked uncertainly.

"Yes," Danielle said. "Now, darling, much as I want to talk to you, I've got to get some sleep. Tracy is recording tomorrow and I've got to be there."

"All right," Jules said, still not convinced that he shouldn't go right back out to the Los Angeles airport and catch the night flight to New York. "Don't let that spoiled brat give you any trouble," he said angrily. "If he does, let me know and I'll put the fear of God into him."

"There won't be any trouble," Danielle said quickly. "He's fine. He'll record tomorrow and the next day."

"Okay, okay. Remember you don't need him. You can get other clients easily."

"Yes," Danielle said in a small voice.

Then there was a long silence while neither of them knew what to say and the long-distance line hummed between them.

"Good night, Jules," Danielle said finally.

"Good night, baby," he said. "I love you."

"Me, too."

After he had hung up he watched the shadow that the sun made against the pink wall while he tried to dispel the uneasiness he felt from the phone call. A pair of youngsters, teenagers no older than eighteen, went by, the boy with his arm about the waist of the girl. Jules thought of Tracy Harmon, who wasn't that much older than the boy out there carrying his tennis racket with his free hand. He felt angry at the young people with talent who wanted so much and gave so little in their personal relations. That boy out there, who was just disappearing around the corner in the direction of the tennis courts, probably had nothing more to do than go on to college. Somewhere, a rich father behind a big desk like Jules's was planning a law career or a career in the entertainment business for him. Tracy Harmon, like so many of the singers, had gotten his break too young and they were just experienced enough to know that they were only going to get one chance at it.

The phone on the bedside table rang

again and Jules snatched it up, hoping it
was Danielle, but it was one of the executives from Star Records' West Coast office
saying he was in the Polo Lounge, and
asking Jules to come out and have a drink.
Jules agreed, begging for a few minutes to
freshen up. These trips, which to outsiders
looked like such perfect boondoggles—
California, sunshine, the Beverly Hills
Hotel—were in fact fast-moving business
trips for Jules. He doubted he'd get so much
as a moment to lie by the pool in the two
weeks that he'd be away. Perhaps on the
weekend, when he had to travel up the
coast to negotiate a four-record deal with
the agent of Star Records' biggest star, he
might just snatch some time for himself.
By the time he got back to New York he'd
need another vacation himself, but in fact,
he'd have to stay late at the office for another week catching up on what he had missed
while he was away.

With a sigh, he rose and went into the
bathroom. He splashed cold water on his
face and looked at himself in the mirror as
he patted his face dry. The two intense
weeks with Danielle had somehow erased
lines of tension that he had thought were
just naturally part of growing older. Happiness could do that.

He quickly changed into a fresh white

shirt, threw his blazer on again and went through the gardens to the Polo Lounge, where many of the biggest deals in Hollywood had been struck for the last fifty years. He liked Los Angeles. He wasn't one of those New Yorkers who looked down on the town as shallow because everything out there was so attractive and seemingly so easy. This was a hardworking town that had turned out the best film and music of the twentieth century. But he had to admit to himself as he passed one beautiful tan after another, one pastel shirt and pair of perfectly pressed linen slacks after another, that there was a strange element to Hollywood whereby its art had fed back upon itself. It created magic on the screen, but somehow the houses and the people had eventually come to resemble stage sets and actors dressed by costume departments.

His business associate was waiting for him in the Polo Lounge.

"How are you, kid?" Harry Rothman said, standing up and offering his big hand. Harry was a talent discoverer for Star. He traveled the smaller clubs throughout the country looking for that one voice in a hundred thousand. "Don't tell me," he said in answer to his own question. "You look great. You look ten years younger. Only one thing does that: love."

Jules laughed and dropped onto the bench besides Harry. "You're right, Harry," he said.

"Oh, boy," said Harry, who had had four marriages to date and, though he was still an incurable romantic, had begun to have his doubts about whether love and marriage should be connected. "Bring the man a drink," he said jokingly, as he waved a waiter over.

Jules ordered a white wine spritzer because he still had a lot of work to do later and he was still on New York time. "No, Harry," he said when the waiter had gone. "This is different."

"Tell me about her."

Jules did, but when he got to the part about what Danielle did for a living, Harry's face seemed to mottle and he choked on his drink. "A talent manager?" he said, aghast. "You've gotten yourself involved with a talent manager?"

"This is different," Jules said defensively, feeling his own color deepen. He knew that in the industry the music people were considered the flakiest of the lot.

"If I had a buck for every time those words have been spoken in this room,"

Harry said, "I wouldn't need Star Records. No, no," he said, holding up his hand before Jules could protest. "I know the look. The man is blind. I won't say any more. What did you say her name was?"

"Danielle Martins."

Harry's big, bluff face creased. "Danielle Martins," he repeated. "Don't know her."

Jules could see that bothered Harry, who prided himself on knowing anyone who was remotely anyone in the industry. That was how he had gotten his famous leads for Star Records, leads that sent him running off to obscure places and had led to the discovery of some famous performers.

"She only manages Harmon," Jules said.

"Harmon," said Harry, making a sour face.

"I thought he was one of the comers," Jules said.

"Could be," Harry said. "Touch and go right now." Harry seldom spoke ill of anyone and almost never of talent. What he left unsaid told Jules that Harry wasn't at all hopeful of Tracy Harmon's ability to deliver.

"He goes into the studio tomorrow," Jules said.

"Good luck to your friend," Harry said.

Then they talked about the business that Jules had come to the Coast to handle.

Jules listened with half a mind as Harry outlined the latest developments. He couldn't entirely get rid of the uneasy feeling that the phone call to Danielle had brought on. He thought of her back in New York in her apartment. He conjured up the apartment in his mind and imagined Danielle in bed with her dark hair thrown out on the pillow. His body responded to that image and he found himself lifting his hand to his mouth in a gesture he had come to use a lot over the last weeks: no matter how carefully you showered, he knew that when you slept in close contact with a person for days at a time, there was always some last lingering fragrance of them on your skin.

But the heavily fragrant soap of the hotel seemed to have wiped that away from his hands, and again he felt a quick sense of loss as though by leaving Danielle alone, he was losing her.

"You following, Jules?" Harry asked.

"Sorry, Harry. Mind wandered a bit there. Tired I guess," Jules apologized. "Time difference."

He hadn't convinced Harry, Jules saw, but the other man made no further reference to Jules's attention wandering and they concluded their business.

Harry said, "You want to get a bite to eat?"

"No, I don't think so, Harry," Jules said. "I think I'll order something from room service and hit the sack."

"Good man," Harry said. He slapped Jules on the back and lifted his hand for the check.

Jules watched the deal makers as they huddled over their drinks. He distracted himself from his worries by trying to figure out at which point of the deal each table was: The two men and the stunning red-haired woman at the table nearby must be an actress, her agent, and a producer. Jules was willing to bet the man leaning back in his chair was the producer, and the man holding on to the stem of his glass as though it were a lifeline, the agent. And the pair at the next table, the two women, neither that young but both dressed in designer label clothes. What were they talking about, interrupting each other as they were in a rapid stream of intense talk? Divorce, most likely. Jules was willing to bet it wouldn't be a new experience for either, with marriage out here, where the bucks were so high, having become almost an industry in itself.

Harry interrupted this train of thought by standing up. Jules led him out to the front door to wait while his car was brought around by a car boy. The boy first brought a

Rolls-Royce, two Porsches and a Mercedes sports car; then Harry's own dark brown Mercedes town car, which cost what a house in a small town would, lumbered to an imposing stop under the green canopy.

The money, Jules reflected as he saw Harry sail down the winding driveway and out onto the Sunset Strip, was so extraordinary in this business. Could you blame people for all the things they did to break into the industry and stay there?

Back in the room again, Jules found that he was indeed exhausted. He picked up the room service menu and called in for a clubhouse sandwich and a tall glass of milk. The voice on the other end, polite to the point of self-effacement, seemed convinced that he would be much happier with a full meal, wine and a liqueur.

While he waited, he showered, wrapped himself in the thick white robe the hotel provided and was just laying out his papers for the morning when there was a discreet knock on his door. He opened it to find a waiter with a trolley draped in a starched white cloth and on it a silver covered dish. Jules wanted to take the sandwich and the glass of milk into the room and leave the trolley outside, but he was too tired to argue and he stood by while the waiter rolled the trolley in, set up the table with silverware and, with a flourish, lifted the silver dish to reveal the four small sections of the clubhouse on a royal blue porcelain plate.

The waiter seemed as shocked as Jules was amused and looked quickly at the check, which Jules signed, adding a generous tip for the surprise.

He took the sandwich to the bed, switched on the television and listened to the news as he ate. When he got up to hang out the Do Not Disturb sign for the maid, he saw that the sun had slipped down in the sky to where it could no longer be seen from the hotel. The gardens were cast in a melancholy twilight that brought its own response from Jules.

Danielle would be asleep by now, her smooth arm wrapped around the pillow that she embarrassedly had gone to her own apartment to get the second night they had slept together.

"My bear pillow," she had said with a small shy smile, holding on to an old down pillow that seemed to have lost half its contents. "It's only a pillow, but I feel about it the way children feel about teddy bears," she admitted.

Jules had put on a stern look. "Any other strange habits?" he had asked. "You better get them out now. I'm not sure I'm up to many surprises like this."

She giggled. "You'll just have to wait and see," she said, walking past him and arranging her poor excuse for a pillow among his own. At the sight of the pillow that meant so much to her huddled among the larger ones that he liked, Jules's heart had filled with unexpected joy.

In the night he had awakened and watched her sleeping, her body curled into his, her face buried in her bear pillow and a smile of contentment on her lips. He loved her and he wanted to keep her safe all her life. Those were his thoughts, and they were solemn thoughts that meant rearranging large parts of what he had planned for himself, but he wanted to for her, for them. He had lain awake in the dark with her body against his, thinking about the new future that had appeared like an island out of a clear tropic sea offering new discoveries.

Now he wanted to call Danielle again and wake her, but that was the behavior of an adolescent. He wanted to say good night to her and know that his world was safe.

He turned out the lights and picked up the phone. The impulse to call was strong, but instead he called the front desk and asked them to hold all calls. The time was still early there, though L.A., with its six A.M. studio calls, was an early town, closing softly like a hibiscus blossom at the end of the day.

He fell asleep instantly and then, in what seemed but minutes, awakened with his heart pounding as though he had run a fast race. He lay looking at the dark ceiling, and the feelings that came now were not love for Danielle but anger at Beth for all the emotional flotsam she had left in the wake of her departure.

He was soon asleep again, a fitful sleep where Beth, who had been gone from his dreams for a long time, drifted through and they embraced. She was gone, and Danielle was there walking across a dark hillside hand in hand with him. Then she was gone and when he awoke he was bathed in sweat.

He looked at his watch. Six A.M. Nine in New York. He lifted the telephone and put the call through with his heart racing again, and when Danielle lifted it and said hello, relief rushed through him.

"It's me," he said almost sullenly in his embarrassment.

"Hello, you," Danielle said. "Is everything all right?"

"No," he said. "I want you to come out here, this weekend."

He could hear her thinking.

"All right," she said slowly. Then after

another long pause, "Tracy finishes taping on Friday I think, unless there's some last mixing to be done. I could catch the late flight."

"Do that," he said.

The long silence that now stretched between them brought back all his worries from the earlier conversation. "Are you all right?" he asked.

"I miss you," she said. But it was as though she were holding something back.

"Let's not do this again," he said. "I hate being away from you."

"I love you," she said, and his heart leaped like a spring lamb.

"I'll see you Friday," she said. "I have to get to the studio, darling. Tracy will be pacing and making everybody crazy."

"Friday, then."

He hung up and lay back, happy once more. Watching the sun rise over the square pink corner of the hotel, golden and perfect, bathing the world in warmth, he thought that perhaps paradise was possible after all. He had thought so once, and then for a long time he hadn't, and now he did once again.

Chapter Seven

$\mathcal{D}$anielle came through the gate swinging her blue canvas overnight bag. She wore a white linen jacket over a black skirt and a red silk blouse. Her hair was tied with the same blue and gold scarf she had worn on the day they'd spent in the country. As she moved, her high spiked black heels gave a swing to her hips that had the attention of all the men following behind her.

The sight of her reminded Jules of what it was like to be away from someone you love and then meet them and feel so absolutely right that nothing seems likely to ever go wrong again. He took her in his arms and crushed his lips on hers, and he could feel her giggling under his lips until her own fire caught and they embraced in the center of the airport like teenagers in a drive-in.

Danielle stepped away breathless. "You do sweep a woman off her feet," she said.

Jules bent and picked her up, and she laughed and said, "Jules, put me down right this second." They were the center of attention now, and an appreciative laugh swept through the reception area. They went hand in hand to the baggage area, Jules swinging the overnight bag.

"God, it's good to see you," he said with relief in his voice.

"I don't vanish," Danielle said. "I'm not made of air," and she kissed him on the cheek.

A small burst of applause made them turn, and a man and a woman who had followed them down from the arrival gate were laughing.

"Okay, okay, folks," Jules said, holding up his hands in apology. "We promise to stop making a public display of ourselves."

The couple laughed again and gave a victory sign to Jules, then went to claim their baggage.

"I think I know what it's like to be a celebrity and be public property," Danielle said.

"You better not be public property," Jules said. "I'm staking my claim."

"What an out-of-date chauvinist you are," Danielle said, hugging his arm tight.

"Complaining?"

"No."

They stood together in silent happiness waiting for the baggage to come up the chute. When it did, Jules grabbed Danielle's maroon leather suitcase and they went out into the warm California night. Limousines were lined up three deep in front of the terminal, and across the street the restaurant rose like a flying saucer with spider legs.

Danielle said, "It really is another world, isn't it? You forget when you're away for a while."

"Fantasy land," Jules said.

"Reality's just fine with me," Danielle said, kissing the nape of his neck where it showed at the open collar of his shirt.

"Well, I have one small fantasy surprise," Jules said.

"What?"

"Wait, wait," he said. He led her across the street and into the parking garage. He'd parked as near as he could to the terminal. "There," he said.

She burst into laughter. "Oh, no, Jules," she said. "For us."

"I always wanted one and never could afford one, so . . ." He stood back and admired the red Corvette that sat like an elongated needle in front of them. "Leased," he hastened to assure her.

"Then I'm just glad I thought of this," Danielle said, taking her suitcase from Jules. She put it on the hood of the long red car and snapped open the latches. There on top were Jules's old work jeans and his equally snappy cowboy boots. "I let myself into the apartment," she said.

He pressed his body against hers and bent her slightly backward over the car as he placed his lips again on hers. The fire that ran through his body found a response in Danielle, and he could feel her press against him in her own need. "You are a perfect woman, you know," he told her when they broke apart a minute later. "I don't know why you are still free."

Her green eyes were glazed as she looked up at him, and she said nothing for a long moment. Finally she said, "Oh, Jules, I missed you," and the eyes watered into two bright emerald pools.

He took her in his arms again and they kissed for a long time while their bodies cried out to each other.

It was Jules who was breathless when they parted. He stood back and shook his head as though he had been hit. "Santa Barbara is ninety minutes away," he said. "I don't know if I can wait."

"Well we certainly won't be pulling off to the side of the road like teenagers," Danielle laughed, looking at the sports car.

"There's something wrong with all fantasies, I guess," Jules admitted.

Danielle's face changed slightly, the laughter faded and she looked serious. "I guess," she said, examining his face as though she were checking to see if she remembered every detail.

Jules said, "You are going to see the impossible done before your very eyes. This is, after all, the land of illusion."

"What are you going to do?" Danielle asked suspiciously.

Jules picked up his old jeans and his boots. "I'm going to change my pants in a Corvette."

"Oh, Jules!" Danielle protested.

He kicked off his shoes, opened the door of the car and slid into the driver's seat. "Stand guard," he told her.

He had trouble with his belt buckle, but after that it was clear sailing, sliding out of his lightweight gray slacks. He threw them over the back of the seat onto the ledge behind while Danielle stood trying to hide as much of him as possible. Getting into the jeans was another matter, and as he got one leg on, then couldn't get into the other, Danielle's laughter rose. When he finally had them on and stood up out of the car, he looked as though he'd run a hundred-yard dash.

"You look very cute, cowboy," Danielle said, brushing a lock of his hair off his forehead.

"Whew," he said. He stepped into the boots and pulled them on. "Ta-da!" he announced. "New man."

"The old one looked pretty good," Danielle said, her eyes dancing with laughter.

"What a forward woman you are," Jules said.

"It's we cowgirls," she said. "We learn to take what we want."

Jules snapped the suitcase shut and put it in the trunk. He held the door open for Danielle. "Western courtesy," he told her.

Inside the car he said, "I have to say it. You look great."

"You're prejudiced."

"Right."

"I like that," she said.

Jules turned on the ignition and the Corvette throbbed into life. He could feel Danielle's amusement without even looking at her. "It's going to be perfect," he said.

When she didn't reply he looked at her, and she was watching him with wide, solemn eyes. "It would be nice," she said, and he could hear the same strange overtones that he had heard on the telephone at the beginning of the week. They had spoken during the week, but always for short periods, and only at the end of the day. Often a business dinner would keep Jules too far from the telephone when it was still early enough in New York to call.

He laid his hand on her knee. "Wonderful things do happen," he told her. "Believe. For me."

"Okay, Jules," she said, but the doubt was there.

Jules drove them out into the starlit Western night. He loved driving, and the California freeways always made him feel a freedom he never felt in the East. He turned on the radio and found a country music station. Danielle reached over and he took her hand, driving effortlessly with one hand through the nighttime freeway traffic that lined the San Fernando Valley. Soon they were out of the valley and the coastline appeared on their right, houses dotted along the shore, their lights hinting at other lives being lived quietly on this far edge of the continent. New York seemed a long way away, a lifetime, another place, another time.

The fragrance of Danielle's perfume filled the small interior of the car. Jules stole a glance at her. Her profile was a pale cameo in the dark. "We could leave all this," he said abruptly.

"Jules," she whispered. "Please don't."

"I mean it," he said. "I don't need to be a lawyer for my ego. You don't need trouble like Tracy Harmon. We could charter the *Sapphire* out and live on board her."

"Oh, Jules," Danielle said wistfully. "I love your dreams."

"Dreams come true if you believe hard in them," Jules insisted, stating his own belief, which had seemed to vanish for a long while and now was back like some lost diary, found in an attic, that told you of long-ago hopes.

Danielle squeezed his hand gently. "I hope so, darling," she said with a catch in her voice. "I hope so."

"They will," Jules insisted. "I promise you."

"But let's not talk about them now," Danielle said. "They . . ." Jules waited while she searched in her mind for the words, but when she spoke the words were from her heart. "They hurt too much if you talk about them and they don't happen."

The lights of the drilling platform out in the channel glowed out of the dark, a pirate ship alight in the night. The *Sapphire* would be in St. Thomas now, Jules thought. The two boys who had taken her down would have her scrubbed down and ready for him when he had the time to get down there. Alone he would have flown down half a dozen times during the winter, sometimes with a companion but at least as often by himself. He loved the solitude of the open sea, the long stretches of water ahead and the sails billowing with wind above. He wanted to be alone on his boat with Danielle, the two of them together with the world fresh and new about them.

"Why am I behaving like such a child?" he asked her.

"Because you're special," she told him.

He looked at her quickly to see if he'd heard right.

"All the special people have it, I think," she said. "The leftover beliefs of their childhood. I think it is wonderful you still have it. Most people lose that. It's called maturity. I don't think maturity is all it's cracked up to be."

Jules had never discussed Beth with Danielle. He had seen so many of his friends, when one affair was over, make a career of discussing it with every person who came along later. Beth and he had the dignity not to drag out all their memories, good and bad, for everyone to pass through. And particularly with Danielle he hadn't wanted the old ghosts leaning over their shoulders to listen to their private thoughts and words. He wanted the world new for them.

"You're mature," he said thoughtfully.

"I've had to be," she said, and he waited, wondering if this was the moment she would speak of the past, but she said nothing else.

Soon the lights of Santa Barbara appeared in a diamond crescent far ahead, and Jules said, "Hungry?"

She shook her head. "I just want your arms about me," she said, and suddenly she shivered.

They crested the hill and there below them was the small Spanish-architectured town. A strong fragrance of eucalyptus filled the car as they began the descent, and they could hear the mission bells pealing.

Jules drove along the palm-lined oceanfront drive until they came to the Biltmore Hotel. A car boy dressed in a red jacket came running across the velvet-soft grass before the sound of the engine had died in the night.

They stepped out into a silence like the ocean depths. The car boy took the red Corvette away, breaking the silence with a roar, and bellboys appeared from the golden interior of the lobby. They followed them across a floor of large square red tiles scattered with rich Oriental rugs that glowed under the light of the brilliant chandeliers high above. A small orchestra was softly playing dance music in one of the rooms off the lobby.

"This is like a very large private house," Danielle said, dropping her voice low.

"Yes," Jules said.

Two couples in evening clothes appeared and seemed to glide across the floor toward the sound of the music.

"It's like another time," Danielle said.

"No," Jules said. "It's today. These are the hidden people. They live on in their own way ignoring the present. Sailors are like that too."

A bellboy led them through a silent moon-lit garden to a cottage near the back of the hotel. The door had hardly closed behind him when Jules took Danielle in his arms and kissed her.

"We could change and go to dinner," he said. "Or . . ."

"I like the sound of 'Or,'" she murmured.

Now he leaned down and swept her up into his arms and carried her across the room into the bedroom. She reached up her arms and put them around his neck, and as she pulled him toward her, he heard her kick off her shoes. He lowered them both onto the bed, where she sat up and pulled the scarf from her hair. When she shook her head the mass of dark curls fell about her face.

Jules put his hand up and stroked the soft cheek. She sat beside him, one arm on his chest, and looked into his eyes. "Are your intentions honorable?" she asked.

He shook his head.

"Not one?" she whispered, a small smile playing about her mouth.

"Not tonight," he said.

She began to unbutton his shirt until she could reach in and play her hand on his chest. She ran her hand over his chest, smoothing out his chest hair, and then laid her cheek on his bare flesh. Jules put his hand on her back and began to run it softly up and down. She began to make little sounds of contentment as he kissed the top of her head.

Danielle raised her head, tossing her froth of curls out of her face. "I can't believe I met you," she murmured.

"Stealing your newspaper," he said. Their limbs were entwined. They might as well have been one person, Jules thought.

"Ah, you finally admit it," she said.

"Right now I'd say anything," he teased her.

She started to unbutton his shirt further, and when she came to his belt he reached forward to help. She slapped his hand gently and gave him a smile of such wickedness that he raised both his eyebrows at her. She undid his belt and the top buttons of his jeans, and he felt a heat run through him as she smoothed her hand over the pebbled muscles of his stomach. Now it was his turn to make small noises of contentment.

"Danielle," he murmured, and he reached for her and took her in his arms while their mouths searched feverishly for each other. They undressed with passionate abandon, dropping their clothes wherever they fell. Jules cupped his hands under Danielle's full breasts and placed his lips on each in turn, running his tongue about the nipples while she reached for the back of his head, holding his face between her breasts, calling his name softly as though he were far off on an open sea and she the siren of the shore.

Their passion rose together and they could wait no longer. She said, "Please, Jules, now . . . Jules . . ."

He pulled himself above her and she clutched at his darkly tanned shoulders; her legs came about him as he entered her, her body arched and then they were one again, brought together after too long a parting. They found each other's secret rhythm, holding to each other with a desperation as they searched for some final closeness that would make them each other's forever. They called to each other with voices choked with the sobs of mutual need until they were spent, unwilling to separate, lying together, holding to the moment when they had been one even as it passed away into memory.

They dropped into a sleep that was almost a coma, still wrapped together, and when Jules awoke, moonlight bathed the carpet. He lay holding on to Danielle, listening to her even breathing, enjoying the sense of security and well-being that her presence had brought.

"Are you awake?" she whispered.

"Yes." Their words seemed to fall into the silence of the room like pebbles into the stillness of a pool, leaving ripples that faded into silence.

"I love you, Jules," Danielle said softly. "I always will."

The tears stung Jules's eyes and he drew a deep breath. His flesh lay lightly against hers. A crescent moon moved imperceptibly in the night sky outside the window while stars floated above the ocean.

"I wonder what time it is," Danielle said after a while.

"I have a terrible confession to make," Jules said.

He felt her heart miss a beat against his chest and felt a sense of guilt. "What?" she asked, tension in her voice.

"I'm starved," he said languidly, and was rewarded for his teasing by a vicious pinching of his cheek.

"Beast," she said.

"Man may not live by bread alone, but it helps."

Danielle's own stomach rumbled in answer.

"Ah," he said. "You accuse me, and you're hungry too!"

"Ravenous," she admitted, sitting up. Her breasts were firm, framed against the moonlit window, her back a graceful curve above him.

He reached for her.

She leaped back. "Oh no," she said. "You started this."

"Love is like Chinese food," he began, and got in return a good swift kick that sent him sprawling on the carpet beside the bed.

"To the showers," she ordered him.

Jules pulled on his jeans again and buttoned his shirt loosely above them, then left the bedroom to Danielle. He went out into the living room, checking his watch which he had found on the floor. It was nearly ten.

He called the desk and asked them to re-
serve a table in the dining room in forty-five
minutes and to send a bottle of chilled
champagne to the room.

He lit the fire and sat by himself, looking
at the flames as they rose and fell back in
the small fireplace. He hadn't known, how
tense he had been until Danielle had arrived. He could feel the week's tension
going, the muscles unknotting in his neck,
his pulse slowing down.

The champagne came, and when the
waiter had gone, Jules popped the cork and
poured two glasses into the crystal goblets
the hotel had provided.

He carried them into the bathroom,
where Danielle sat up to her neck in bubbles in a vast old-fashioned bathtub raised
on four clawed feet.

"Crystal?" she said, looking at the carved
glass when he handed it to her.

"Only the best. These are the lost people.
They live in another world."

"Shangri-La," Danielle said, holding her
glass up so he could touch it with hers.

The glasses touched with a small bell-
like sound. "Except it's real." Jules said.
"This world exists. You just have to reach
for it."

She sipped on her champagne and her
eyes watched him closely. She had tied her

hair back with a green velvet ribbon and the mass of curls had tightened in the steam that rose from the scented bath.

"We have a table in forty-five minutes," he said.

Danielle sipped on her glass and handed Jules a sponge. He put down his glass and plunged the oversized sponge into the soapy water. She leaned forward, holding her hair higher with one hand while he spread the bubbles over the soft flesh of her back, across the shoulders first and then in circles, moving the sponge with one hand and following with the rougher skin of his other sun-browned hand, making a path across the pink flushed skin until he could feel the gentle curve below the water where her hips flared from her waist.

Danielle reached behind her and took his hand and held it against her cheek. She lay back in the bath and her breasts broke the surface of the bubble-frothed water. He took each of them in turn and soaped them while her neck arched back in a perfect smooth curve and her thick lashes fell shut across her limpid eyes.

When he stopped, she opened them, her eyelids lifting in one swift movement.

Jules leaned down and kissed her, and she put her soft hands beneath his shirt and held him by his strong shoulders.

When they broke from their kiss, Jules sat on the rim of the bathtub and they looked at each other for a long silent moment.

He stood up without a word and went out, leaving the door open behind him. The bedroom was bright with the moonlight now, and he bent to light a fire in the bedroom fireplace. He poured more champagne for himself and drank it silently, looking through the narrow window at the velvet-soft lawn while he listened to Danielle finish her bath in the other room.

"Yours, darling," she said, coming in toweling her hair. She picked up her empty glass, which Jules had brought with him, and poured herself another glass.

Jules went into the bathroom, dropped his clothes on the floor and stepped into the big glass shower stall in the corner. The water came out forcefully and hot, and he soaped himself down. He followed with a brisk, icy shower and stepped into the white-tiled bathroom, again filled with new energy.

The bedroom door was closed. He took the lightweight dark suit he'd brought with him and a crisp white shirt and dressed quickly, then opened the door to the bedroom with his shirt still open and his necktie trailing in his hand.

Danielle stood against the fireplace in a short evening dress of peach chiffon. She came toward him and took the tie from his hand. Standing in front of him, she put the tie around his neck. Her fragrance wafted about him as she pulled the tie through his collar and tied it slowly, her eyes never leaving his.

"I don't like to think of where you learned to tie a man's tie backward without looking," he murmured.

"My father," she said briskly, losing credence by giving him a slow wink.

"That does it," he said as she stepped back and poured him the last of the champagne and handed it to him. "I can't ever let you go."

They drank to that, and then Jules put the fire screen in front of the glowing fire and they went out into the warm California night.

The hotel rose ahead of them like a fairy palace shining with light. They went through to the dining room, where half the tables were still occupied with diners, all beautifully dressed.

Danielle whispered, "I'm glad I took the trouble to dress properly."

"Understatement of the year," Jules said dryly.

"Oh, this man says the nicest things,"

Danielle told a startled maitre d' in a tuxedo, who had appeared carrying menus with the aplomb of Moses carrying the Ten Commandments.

The maitre d' led them to a table at the edge of the small dance floor while the six-piece orchestra slowed to change tempo into a waltz. Jules took Danielle in his arms and, with a nod to the maitre d' who stood by holding out a chair for Danielle, danced her smoothly onto the floor among the half dozen couples who were gliding by. They caught each other's rhythm instantly and they became one person moving to the music that seemed to come from within them. Her steps followed his, her body responded to his touch and when they came back to their table some minutes later, they felt almost as though they had made love again.

"More champagne?" Jules asked.

"I don't know whether it's the wine or something else," Danielle said, "but I feel as though I'm in another world."

A happiness had descended upon them that was so complete it required no words. They ordered a meal and sat holding hands across the table, listening to the music and watching the dancers, who seemed, as they swept around the room, like extras hired to perform.

Jules felt Danielle's hand squeeze his lightly, and he looked across the table to see her gazing at him with a love so deep he felt the shock go right through him.

"This doesn't happen in real life," she said.

"Real life is highly overrated," he told her.

She sighed. "I wish I could believe this could go on forever," she said, and Jules felt a chill pass through the room like the first hint of a storm far from land.

"It can," he said.

"Oh, Jules." The words were filled with their own sadness. Again Jules wondered what lost territory in her past had been so peopled with demons. How could a woman so lovely and young, with such potential for happiness, still be haunted by them?

Then their waiter arrived and they ate quietly while the room slowly emptied until finally they were alone, the waiters standing dutifully about the room with old-world courtesy, their white linen serving napkins draped over their arms and the orchestra still playing quietly.

"I feel I'm alone in a huge palace," Danielle said.

"You deserve a palace," Jules told her.

They were finished, and the waiter merely asked their cabin number and glided off.

Jules stood and took Danielle's arm and the orchestra played them to the door. And as the heavy doors closed behind them, the music faded like a song on the wind. The hotel was empty as they walked through and out into the gardens. The crescent moon hung lower in the sky, moving on its journey toward the other side of the world, and the stars pulsed with their diamond-bright light.

Jules and Danielle walked hand in hand through the mixed fragrance of gardenia and orange blossoms, eucalyptus and freshly mown grass, and Jules heard Danielle draw a deep breath and then shudder. He put his arm about her and held her close to his side.

The scent of burning cedar warmed the cabin though the fires had died to glowing embers. Danielle kicked off her shoes as she came to the old Oriental rug that flowed blood red between the chairs. She dropped onto the sofa and Jules came to her, and they embraced wordlessly, softly, home in each other's arms. Together they watched the embers in the fire die down, and almost without noticing it, like sleepy children, they fell asleep in each other's arms.

Chapter Eight

The sun reflected off the water. Out in the channel the oil derricks were delicate lace constructions rising from the ocean floor. A flotilla of sailboats bent their white fins into the wind, and in the distance the islands were a pale green smear against a tangerine sky.

Danielle sighed. "I don't want to go home," she said.

They hadn't talked about New York. The weekend had seemed to evaporate about them, time passing swiftly, moment by moment, as they drank in each other's company like parched travelers through a burning desert.

"I'll be back in a week," Jules said.

They were walking along the beach. A dog bounded down the slope from the cliffs that rose up to their right, prancing out onto the hot sand with his ears flying.

"I feel the way he does," Danielle said, indicating the dog. "I want to run and jump and just let the world know how happy I am."

Jules squeezed her hand. In two days he had been drawn closer to Danielle than he had ever been to any human being. It was as though they had known each other for a long time instead of less than a month.

"When will the taping be over?" he asked. The sight of the sailboats tacking in the wind had brought on a pang of longing to show Danielle the beautiful black hull of the *Sapphire*, his pride and joy.

Danielle blinked and turned to look at the sun with her long lashes half-closed over her bright green eyes. "This week," she said. She hadn't spoken about the taping, and Jules hadn't pried because he didn't want to think about Tracy Harmon. He didn't want to share their time together, his and Danielle's, with anyone, not even the shadows of their other lives.

"Are you pleased with what you're getting?" he asked her now.

She didn't reply at first, and for a moment Jules thought she might not have heard. "He's working hard," she said finally.

"And?"

Danielle turned to face him. The two days of sun had dusted her cheeks with a light tan highlighting the rich sable of her hair and the brilliant emerald of her eyes. "He's scared," she said.

Jules understood that. "It's the last chance at the gold ring," he said.

Danielle was still looking at him. "Yes," she said.

They walked on a few steps and Jules watched a hawk swoop out of the cliffs, wings wide, and catch a current of air, planing off across the silver sea.

"He's uptight," Danielle said.

Jules could feel that she was holding something back from him. He didn't want to talk about Tracy Harmon. For a moment all his old resolutions about not mixing business with pleasure came back to him, but he dismissed them quickly.

Still he sighed before he spoke. "You know, baby," he said, "I know how you feel about this because Harmon's your client and I respect that, but it's not your responsibility in the final analysis. I mean, we've all opened the door for him and now it's up to him to reach for the ring. You can't hold his hand any longer. You can't put down the songs for him on the tracks. If he doesn't have what it takes . . ."

Jules left unsaid what would happen to Tracy Harmon if he couldn't cut the tracks and record a high-selling record. He would drop away into a small, bitter pool of talent that had had their chances and failed. All their lives they would blame themselves or others. The sadness was worse because, though they could go on to find happiness in other ways, most of them wouldn't, and they would stop their lives—what they considered their real lives—at twenty or twenty-one, as if nothing mattered once their careers in music had stopped. They were has-beens before they knew anything of the true possibilities that life had to offer them.

"He's so young," Danielle said.

Jules could feel the tension in her. He put his arm about her shoulders, but for once she didn't lean against him. Irrationally, a rush of anger went through him, anger at Harmon, at the business. He felt Danielle was being taken from him. He walked on telling himself to be an adult, and then he said as evenly as he could, "Danielle, if he doesn't make it, you can get other clients. You're good, you must be if you've handled Harmon, from all I've heard of him."

As Jules said the words, the *Sapphire* came into his memory again and a dream from the night before of the Caribbean Sea and him and Danielle together. He knew he didn't want Danielle working and he knew that was selfish. He hadn't spoken of it to her and he wouldn't, but the image wouldn't leave.

"He's *got* to make it," Danielle said suddenly. "He's *got* to."

The anger came back to Jules and he dropped his arm from her shoulder. He walked on beside her without saying a word, and then she came to him and put her arm through his. "I'm sorry," she said.

He nodded in understanding. "I love you for your caring," he said. "And I'm still jealous of anything that takes you away from me."

"And I love you for that," Danielle said, the smile he loved so much rising to her lips.

"I'm possessive," he warned her.

She shrugged. "I never could understand why that was considered so awful."

The sun reflecting off the beige sandstone cliffs warmed their faces as they walked down the beach. Something important had happened in their time together, Jules felt, and the happiness that spread through him was like the sun on his skin. He watched a small child leaning over in the ankle-deep water, looking with a tense concentration at the water that swirled about her ankles. A world he had lost had appeared once again before him and a gratitude overflowed within him.

"My plane's at five," Danielle said regretfully.

Jules knew that she had to get back that night because the taping would continue the next morning in New York, but still his heart responded on its own to her reminder. The sun seemed suddenly to sink lower in the sky and lose some of its warmth.

He drew another breath, and then as they walked on he realized that he needed the time to himself next week anyway. He didn't feel bad that he had endured once more all the pangs and jealousies of passion. That was part of love, he supposed, rediscovering the world afresh. Each love was in itself a first love if you were lucky. But he felt that he and Danielle had somehow come to an unspoken understanding that weekend, and now the time had come for them both to accept what they had begun. That would mean change for both of them.

"What are you thinking?" Danielle asked.

"Why?" he teased her with a smile.

"You looked so distant," she said.

"I was thinking I love you."

Her face became solemn, and he saw that she was overcome by an emotion of her own that she was reluctant to let free. "I wish life were simpler," she said when she spoke.

Jules had been thinking something similar a moment before, that love, however strong and straightforward it appeared, was complex and required adjustments. They might have been behaving irresponsibly that weekend, but the truth was that love between them would require special tending to endure.

Yet he said, not wanting to agree that all love has difficulties, "It can be."

Danielle sighed.

"Believe me," he told her.

"I do," she said, and he had to turn away to hide his satisfaction at hearing those two little words that one day soon he hoped to hear her say again in another place.

Chapter Nine

Rain lashed the windows of the jet as it banked for the final approach to Kennedy Airport. In the distance the spire of the Chrysler Building pierced the fog that shrouded the city. Jules felt the race of energy he always felt when he returned to Manhattan, but today he felt more: Danielle was down there in the magic city.

His trip had gone on longer than he had expected. Sometimes he wondered why lawyers didn't finally accept that everything would take longer: If the opposition lawyers told him two weeks, they meant four, and everyone should know it by now. He had expected to be away for two weeks and he had been gone nearly a month. The weekend in Santa Barbara had become a fond memory that he had turned over again and again in his mind, savoring every moment of the time he and Danielle had been able to steal together.

Tallulah had kept him up-to-date on the Tracy Harmon taping. "The kid's slow," she had told him. "Nothing's sparkling, Jules." Jules could hear the concern in Tallulah's voice. Any time that Tallulah actually could put a face and body to a voice, they became her own personal concern, and Jules knew that, having once met Harmon in his office, she was now worried.

Jules had wanted to bring it up with Danielle as gently as he could when she was out on the coast, but every time he had approached the subject, nothing had been resolved. So he had left it alone, letting her tend to her business herself.

After Danielle had gone back to New York, Tallulah called late one night. "Jules?"

"Yeah, Tallulah, what's up?" They had their own rules and they never called each other out of office hours except in emergencies.

"It's Harmon," she said.

Jules looked at his watch. By the light thrown by the main building of the hotel he saw it was three o'clock. That was six A.M.

New York time. Tallulah must be really worried. She must have been up all night or she'd have waited until office hours.

"What's he up to?"

"He nearly took the studio apart yesterday," Tallulah said in her worried voice. "He just went crazy, Jules. Started screaming that everything he'd done was . . ." Tallulah's voice hesitated over the word. She had very strong and surprisingly firm rules about vocabulary. "Manure," she edited, "and that it all had to be started again. I'm sorry to phone you like this, Jules, but they didn't call up from the studio until late and then I took the night to think about it."

Jules's mind was racing. He wondered what Danielle was feeling right now. If Tallulah was concerned, then Danielle must be worried half out of her wits.

"Thanks, Tallulah," he said.

"I thought you might get her before she left for the studio," Tallulah said apologetically. She was breaking her own rules in interfering, but she was also thinking about Jules and he loved her for that.

"You're the best, Tallulah."

"Take care, hon," she said before she went off the line.

Jules lay on his back, wondering how he should handle this piece of information. He didn't want Danielle to think that he was watching Harmon any more than he would watch any young, difficult performer they had under contract. He had tried to get her the night before when he'd gotten back to the hotel, but it had been eleven New York time, and when she hadn't answered on the third ring, he'd hung up. There'd been no message for him in his box, either, but that hadn't surprised him. Recording sessions often went all night.

The light shifted, throwing new patterns of tropical leaves on the ceiling above Jules's bed. He wanted Danielle to be independent. But now, if Harmon himself had gone off the track, she would need someone to talk to. He hoped she wasn't afraid to call him, fearing that it might be his duty to the company to pull the plug on the studio time if Harmon's tracks were coming in as garbage.

Life is so complicated, he thought. What has happened to this fine land, where there should be enough food and housing and comfort for everyone, that we have fallen into such a rat race of fear and greed?

Jules rolled out of bed with a sigh and went to look out the window. If it was Danielle's choice to handle this herself then he must let her. The sun was now a rough tangerine in an aqua sky, and soon all the perfect people would start to move about this paradise of a country on the edge of the continent.

Jules had more work to do than he had expected; he felt like throttling his opposite numbers in the negotiation. When he had arrived at the final conference last night after ten days of detailed talks, the contract put in front of him might as well have been written on another planet. He had never seen it before. It was such an old negotiating trick to wait until the last moment, then present demands so outrageous that you had to weigh them against the need to get the deal concluded. In this case, Star Records had booked stadiums and coliseums worldwide for a female singer to do her much-publicized world tour. Now it would be up to Jules to decide if the loss of all the money it had taken to tie up those buildings would be worth breaking this ridiculous document he'd been presented with, or whether he just had to hunker down and try to make the best last-minute deal he could.

He would hunker, he thought with a sigh. Star's own reputation would suffer if he broke the stadium dates, but he vowed that the next time the lady wantd something out of Star, whether it was a free publicity picture or the key to the ladies' room, it would cost her plenty.

And that, he told himself as he stood by

the window of his cabin, was how the rat race got started.

So he went into the shower after calling room service, and he kept his worries to himself. Danielle was a thinking adult, he tried to remind himself, though every time he did, all he saw was that mass of sleep-tossed hair on his pillow and the lashes that shaded her smiling eyes.

He wanted her with him. He wanted her never to be away from him. This was too tough a business for her, he said to himself as he soaped his body down vigorously. Let anyone be free and independent if they wanted, but was it so bad to want to care for a person so much that you didn't want them hurt or bruised by a lot of spoiled, talented brats?

Danielle had nothing to prove to him, he hoped. All he wanted to prove to her was that he loved her and that he would do his best to keep both of them safe.

He went through to the bedroom, dragging the bath towel. He threw it on the bed impatiently. Then he caught a glimpse of himself in the full-length mirror. His body was strong, his shoulders heavy with muscle and his legs sturdy. He knew with some other part of his mind that he was an attractive man, attractive enough that he didn't need to work his looks the way he saw so many men do—the flashing smile, the chest half-revealed. And he was proud in private that he did still have this fine, manly body, a body hewn from true exercise: these days, it was working on the boat and playing squash; when he was in high school, doing the garden work around the house, chopping the firewood from the trees that he and his father cleared from the back acreage of the Maryland property.

And when he looked at himself, he saw Danielle's pale, smooth body as it had lain against his in the shadowed room of the cabin in Santa Barbara with the firelight reflected through the open door and the sheets tossed like crumpled newspapers at the end of the bed.

What he truly wanted, he thought as he stared at his naked figure, was someone— no, Danielle—to grow old with. Someone who would treasure him as he treasured her and to whom he could give his body and all the rest of him completely and in trust. Someone he could watch as age came, leaving its gentle lines, its reminders as the flesh changed that they were both of them, the lovers, part of the long, real progress of life and that every line or loss was not a loss but merely a marking of the passing of time together.

"You fool," he told himself, smiling at his

reflection. The light was full in the room now, and for the first time he noticed the silver hairs at his temples. He couldn't wait to show Danielle that. "Don't wait too long," an old Blossom Dearie song wafted through his mind, a love song telling one lover not to hesitate because, even as they stood there, time was passing. Then he dressed in the second of the two suits he'd brought with him for the two-week trip. They had gone in and out of the overnight cleaners at the hotel so often they were like guests themselves. He was as tired of them as he was of the perfection that he now saw about him in the gardens as he left his cabin. He was disgruntled and worried and he wanted something imperfect to cross his path. Right then a wide-grinned dog that clearly had an ancestry that no one would ever trace came bounding by and lifted his leg on a well-trimmed bay tree.

"Good boy," Jules said, bending to pat the dog.

The dog accepted the pat and then went off full of confidence into the inner recesses of the well-groomed gardens.

"An omen," Jules said to himself, looking up into the gold and lapis lazuli sky.

He felt much better.

The omen seemed to hold, too, for though Jules forced himself not to call Danielle, knowing she would be under intense pressure, good old Tallulah kept him up-to-date.

"He's got it," Tallulah finally said with the sense of wonder in her voice that she reserved only for talent. "The tapes are . . ." For Tallulah to be without a word was like a New Yorker to be without a subway token hidden somewhere about him. ". . . they're magic, Jules."

Magic. The word was cropping up everywhere like a spell whose time had come. He was happy for Danielle, and he knew that the ironic part of the performing business would now strike and make her, for a while at least, just as nervous as when Harmon wasn't performing: she and Harmon would be breathless with wonder about whether he could keep it up. These golden moments sometimes came and then turned to dross right in front of everyone's eyes. Worse, turned to dross in front of a full studio orchestra and all the technicians watching from the booths. All of them were deeply committed to the business, boosters of talent, and if the performer started to lose whatever it was that had brought him his golden moment, they would suffer along with him, the silence and tension growing hour by hour as he tried to recapture that one three-minute flight of perfection.

So Jules didn't call.

Tallulah's enthusiasm, however, grew every day. "He's going to hit the top," she told Jules the second week. The sessions were running overtime and the technicians were getting so much on tape that Jules had been asked to okay more studio time. If Harmon had it in his blood now, they could get enough on tape to run another record for next year. He was on a winning streak.

Tallulah said, "Jules, I've never heard anything like this." She spoke with the astonishment of a jaded person who had been thrown back into a world of Christmas. "It's like the voice of an angel."

"The voice of an angel?" Jules asked, skeptical now himself, but he knew that the excitement was real.

Soon the word was out in the industry, and an early tape came as fast as a jet could bring it to the West Coast. Jules went with Harry and sat in a booth at Star's West Coast office and heard the voice: pure, thin and crying out from the speakers like some medieval monk in a cathedral singing unexpectedly of the things of the flesh. It made both Harry and him shiver almost simultaneously, that voice. It was unearthly, experienced, pure and filled with a sadness that in one so young seemed the worst crime of all.

Jules tried to think of the spoiled and

petulant boy who had stamped about his office, and he had to remind himself that you never knew: The outer person was so often not the inner, and the inner Tracy Harmon must have been living a life of pain and pleasure that mere mortals would never know—nor have the right to criticize after this record was released.

"Jesus," Harry said when the tape ran on to the soft hush of silence.

What he meant, Jules knew, was that even if Harmon never recorded another note, another line, then as with Joplin or Hendrix, they would play these songs for years to come.

Jules reached for the phone on the control room wall and quickly dialed the New York office. "I've heard it, Tallulah, the tape. Yeah, he's got it."

"He's like an angel," she said, lost in her own thoughts. "I mean, you've heard about them and you know they can't really exist, and . . . bam, there he is strutting down Broadway."

"Are you drinking in the office, Tallulah?" Jules teased her.

"Go on with you; you'll see when the record comes out in December. People will cry when they hear this boy."

Jules knew she was right. Harmon had that rare quality that no one could mix or

define. He was a star. Jules had seen it
happen only once or twice in his life, a
performance so electrifying that in one moment a young performer was shot right to
the top. That was completely different from
a hit record. Harmon wouldn't do anything
for a while now, Jules suspected. Danielle,
if she was good, would seclude him until
this record was out. There was nothing to
win and a lot to lose. A good manager would
put Harmon on ice, let the word spread,
then, when the record hit, just present her
client as a star, no questions asked.

He was happy for her and yet there was a
sadness there too, and he was honest
enough to know who the sadness was for.

"I love you, Jules," her last words had
been at the Los Angeles airport. "I always
will. I know that," and she had touched his
cheek. He'd wanted to pull her to him. Her
plain denim blouse was open at the neck to
show the full flesh of her tanned breasts
from the days in the sun, and as she turned
away, her hips in their white linen slacks
held all the promise of her ripe young wom-
anhood.

But she had stepped on the moving esca-
lator sidewalk and it began to bear her
away. Jules had walked along beside her,
half trotting as the mechanical sidewalk

took her further into the interior of the terminal. She was laughing at him now. "Only one week, darling," she'd said.

He'd leaned to kiss her, put his hand on the moving rail, and was jerked away from her lips as though by another, darker magic.

The second time their lips touched. "One week," he'd whispered.

"One week," she'd agreed, and he stood back and let the machine bear her away into the distance past the long murals by local schoolchildren.

Harry was standing by his car when they came out of the studio. "I don't know what you did, Jules, but whatever you want, it's yours. We were going to write Harmon off to losses. But that . . ." He gestured back at the studio wall behind them. "That . . . that's religion."

Jules had to blink hard twice to be sure he had heard Harry right. First Tallulah and then Harry, two of the toughest around. There wasn't anything they hadn't seen or heard in this business.

"That comes along once in a lifetime," Harry said. "You're the tops, Jules. When this is over, take some time off and take that boat of yours out, okay?"

But Jules was too lost in his own mind to

respond to Harry's suggestion. A canopy of ice like the return of the glaciers seemed to be creeping toward his heart.

He watched Harry drive away and he got into his own rented car, the one he'd traded in the red Corvette for at the end of his weekend with Danielle. He told himself all the right words, that he was insecure, a fool, that he had to trust Danielle, she wasn't like some of the other people in this industry. Still, when he handed over his car to the boy at the entrance to the hotel, his hands were damp with a cold sweat.

He went right into the Polo Lounge and took a table in the corner near a broad-leaved palm that rose out of a terra cotta planter with so much energy it looked as if it were auditioning for a role in a jungle movie.

"Bring me a telephone," he told the waitress. "Please."

"A drink?" she inquired, looking at him with concern.

He hadn't thought of that, but this was a bar. "Martini," he said, "straight up with a twist." He'd drink to Tallulah with Tallulah's favorite end-of-day drink.

The telephone arrived at the same time as the drink. The girl placed the drink carefully in front of him while a boy dutifully plugged in the phone. Jules took a healthy sip and then picked up the receiver. Quietly he gave the hotel operator the number, then stared out at the room as the call went through with a series of mysterious clicks and snaps.

Danielle's voice came on the line like a benediction. "Hello?"

He couldn't speak for a second. The new emotion was so strange that for a second he began to worry about his own sanity. He felt happiness, anger, and relief wash over him all at once.

"Hello?" she repeated.

"It's me," he said.

"Oh, Jules," she said, and her voice dropped away.

He didn't know what he'd expected, but it wasn't that.

"I had to speak to you."

There was a long silence, and his nervousness increased.

"I'm glad you called," she said finally, and her voice still was distant and flat.

"Danielle?"

She sighed. "I can't really talk now, darling," she said.

He didn't know why it was such a surprise. He knew she had someone else there. He felt at first as though he'd been hit in the solar plexus. All the breath went out of him and the room seemed to slide away from him in a quick movement like a camera pulling back.

Danielle must have understood suddenly what he was thinking. "Tracy's here," she said. And then, "Jules, darling, I can't talk now." She had her hand near the receiver, he knew, shielding her voice from Tracy.

He relaxed, but not before he had another surge of fury that the world was so damned complicated. All he wanted to say to her was "I love you," and all he wanted to hear back from her was "I love you," and the world would be perfect.

If she couldn't speak, he could. "I love you," he said.

The hesitation while she found the right response, meaningful to him but not to her audience, seemed to Jules as long as winter when he was at school. "I believe," she told him, playing back his own words from the weekend.

They rang off awkwardly. She was having as rough a time as he had thought, and for a second he felt guilty at having broken his vows not to call her. But then he was glad he had. He needed her, and he thought from the small catches he heard in her voice that she was lonely also, needing his support, but as usual, too proud to ask. She had been alone a long time. One romance with a man who seemed to love her wouldn't wipe out whatever had come before, the fearful thing that she had never spoken of.

"I believe," she had said. He would have that engraved inside their rings. Yes, he decided, he was going to wear a ring himself. He had never wanted to before, but now he wanted to desperately.

His pleasure rose like a tide in him again at the thought of Danielle in New York, with her sable-rich hair and her slim, broad-shouldered body. He looked at the other women in the lounge, all perfect in their way: a redhead who was so passionate in her very presence she could lead a revolution, a small, tawny-haired woman filled with the animation of talent; and a blonde, so bland and expressionless she might have been billed as "This Year's Blonde." And suddenly he could appreciate all of them in their own very special way because he had Danielle, who might not be as perfect as any of these women but who made his own life take on new importance, new excitement, and—he saw this too—new belief in himself because he was no longer alone.

"Another martini," he told the returning waitress.

She cocked her head at him. I must be grinning like a hyena, he thought. "Good news?" she asked. How do you express having found the secret of life? Jules wondered. He heard himself say, "I'm in love."

"It's curable," she told him with the experience of Hollywood behind her.

"Not this time," he assured her. "Fatal case."

She smiled. "You look like a nice man," she said, and it wasn't a come-on. It was an observation tinged with curiosity.

"That's what I hear."

"Good luck then," she said. "And that won't help much if you're planning on having any more," she said, pointing at the martini.

"Just this one," he assured her.

"Okay," she said, "but I've seen a lot of good intentions slip away with those."

She went off to get him his drink.

Jules enjoyed his second martini quietly. His sense of well-being had returned. A hit record for Tracy Harmon—more than that, stardom—and Danielle as his manager. She would be busy, he knew, but she would also be proud, and there was nothing like achievement to help self-image. He was happy for her.

The bar had filled up and he began to feel self-conscious holding a table to himself. He called for the check from the bright, smiling waitress and signed it, leaving a man-in-love tip that even at Star Records would raise eyebrows. He didn't care. The world was nearly perfect. He didn't know what he had done to deserve it, but a wave of happiness had come to him and he had been ready for it, riding forward like the kids on their surfboards on the beach off the hotel.

"Believe," he had told Danielle, and as he had said it he had known from his own vague uneasiness that it was a command that he too found hard to accept. But he would. He did. He believed in Danielle. And soon he would see her.

Manhattan rose like a floating island out of the mist and fog as the plane circled it, and then the highest part of the lyrical city was gone as the plane dropped into the banks of fog. Beads of rain streaked Jules's window, and he tapped the arm of his seat impatiently.

He could leave his luggage, he thought, and have someone from Star come out and reclaim it tomorrow.

"You schoolboy," he chided himself. "You have to learn to be a dignified older man. You're thirty-four."

Thirty-four. When did that happen? was the thought that flashed through his head as the tires bumped down and, with a sickening lurch, left the tarmac and hit again.

The roar of the engines as they reversed brought a new rush of inevitable anxiety to Jules. Of course the plane would land safely.

He was already off his seat when the stewardess began her recitation to please remain seated until they had come to a complete stop at the terminal.

He forced himself to sit down and decided he'd leave the luggage.

Danielle would be at the apartment if he was lucky. He'd called Tallulah and had her get hold of Danielle in the studio to tell her he was finally coming back. The two weeks had stretched into four, and for the last five days he had thought each day that he would be finished. He'd packed his bag each day at the hotel, hoping that he could just pick them up and rush for the airport, and each day there had been one more clause undecided. And a clause in a record contract could mean millions. The shoelace concession for *E.T.* had gone for a quarter of a million dollars. But there were times in the middle of the night, when he was arguing over a children's lunch box concession, that Jules truly thought he was in a fool's business. Other thirty-four-year-olds were discovering cures for diseases, making useful things like chairs and tables, and he was haggling over the right to put a teenboy's long-haired face on the side of a child's lunch box—and with as much passion as though they were dividing Europe.

Finally the contract had been signed and he'd had the hotel send his luggage in a separate car to the airport while he raced from Star Records' downtown office. He'd caught the nine o'clock flight, midnight New York, which was bringing him in on a rainy foggy dawn.

Sunlight on clear water had never looked as good as that cold wet autumn day, not yet light, which he saw through the narrow window of the plane.

The plane lurched against the ramp that came out to meet it, and Jules was in the aisle with the other red-eyed passengers.

"Welcome to New York," the stewardess tried to tell him, but he was out and walking briskly down the corridor. He went through the terminal at a half trot and out into the wet, cold morning.

The rain felt wonderful on his unshaven cheeks. He raised his hand for the first cab and was in it and giving his destination before the door was shut behind him.

Home. He hadn't known he felt that way about New York. Home had been some far-off memory, the room he stayed in when he went down to Maryland each Christmas, a place where his pennants were still on the

wall, his single bed with the cretonne bed-
spread, his desk finally clear of the clutter
he had kept there when he was growing up.
His mother had wanted to turn it into a
second-floor den, and Jules had urged her
to do so, but somehow it never got done.
And he was always glad, because he could
stand there in that room, breathing in the
lemon polish and other odors that brought
back memories of safe, early days.

New York had been excitement, the chal-
lenge, and when he and Beth arrived it had
seemed to them their own secret, a secret
even that they were *there:* they would conquer and . . . They never went beyond that.
And something else would happen. They
had never thought of it as home, either of
them, not in the best sense of the word.
They were out to make their mark.

Where was she? Jules wondered suddenly as the taxi turned onto the freeway
into the city. He hadn't wondered that
about Beth in a long time. Was she here?
Was she happy? He hoped so. And with that
thought, sitting in the stuffy, humid interi-
or of the cab, he knew that he was finally
free. The bond was broken. He could wish
Beth happiness and he felt a small, be-
grudging shame that he had had to wait so
long to be able to send that silent message

to her. He could wish her happiness in her quest for that other world because he had Danielle.

The pain was gone.

"Bridge or tunnel?" the driver asked.

"You choose," Jules said, anxious to be home. Let the driver make the choice of which route to take. He wouldn't, like so many New Yorkers, try to prove he was smarter than the cab driver. Jules felt like everybody's friend.

Danielle would be asleep, he supposed, and he knew he must smell like a moose after his hard day's work on the other coast, the restless flight across the sleeping nation. Racing in toward the fantasy city that rose ahead out of the mist and rain, its lights from the night still sparkling in the tallest buildings, his body knew that Danielle was close. It had a life of its own, his skin tingling and his blood rushing through him. He wanted her in his arms again, her lips under his. He wanted to caress the soft skin of her flesh.

The driver swung onto the bridge, moving quickly through traffic, and then Jules's city was about him, rising on either side. He watched a garbage truck, its cheerful crew shouting at each other, oblivious to the sleeping people in the buildings. He watched a bleary-eyed man with his coffee cup in his hand walking his dog. Traffic moved at a steady pace through the park, and then they were on the West Side and Jules was fumbling for his wallet.

"Want to hit that sack, huh?" the driver said, looking in the mirror at Jules's exhausted eyes.

"That bad, huh?"

"Seen brighter," the driver said cheerfully. "Welcome home, anyway," he added, taking his fare and the tip.

The night doorman hadn't left. He let Jules in, and Jules went through the lobby looking at the hanging chandelier where the bulbs still sparkled from the night.

Home.

The elevator, drab as it was, seemed to welcome him. He stepped out on the floor where both he and Danielle lived. He went up to her door and pushed the doorbell. A tune was floating in his mind. If he hadn't known better he would have thought he was drunk, but it was merely the happiness of being there outside her door. When she didn't come to the door, he hammered on it softly.

No answer. He put his ear to the door. The silence from within was that of a cloister.

He let himself into his own apartment, which, far from looking welcoming, seemed empty and cold, a reflection of the gray clouds outside the window. He tried the phone, but it rang and rang down the hall with no answer.

She must still be in the studio, he thought. A final recording session with Harmon. But he was sure Tallulah had told him that they had laid down the final track yesterday. Something must have come up, he told himself, a final inspiration of Harmon's to top what was already considered in the corridors at Star to be the greatest gold record since the early Presleys, pure with the purity of the blue mountain country and wise with the street wisdom of the English punkers, one moment in recording history that had, if rumor was true, synthesized a generation's hopes and longings.

The river was a gray line that moved sluggishly in the dawn. A pale sun was trying to break through the mist, but the rain held stubbornly, the downpour growing.

Jules watched a freighter head toward the open sea. The old lady with the torch raised it over the harbor mouth. He was exhausted, he told himself. He should sleep, then try to get into the office later in the day. Danielle would be exhausted too. Tonight, they could have a quick meal and then hold each other and let the true home-coming sweep over them.

The freighter was lost to the mist.

Believe, Jules warned himself. Believe.

Chapter Ten

She was gone.

The rain smearing the windows of Jules's office turned the city outside into a glistening toy. He stood and watched the rain sweep in sheets down the avenue, the hurrying pedestrians bent under their multicolored umbrellas.

An old saying from some past time came to his mind. "A man who is hurt once is sad, a man who is hurt twice is compassionate, but a man who is hurt a third time is a fool."

He felt nothing. His body seemed to belong to someone else. And in his mind he knew that there was still one last part that held on to the dream, one last part that refused to believe.

He turned to look at the package on his desk, long, slim, the box silver, and tumbling from it, the crisp white tissue paper that had wrapped the single red rose.

The card lay by the flower. "Forgive me, please," in Danielle's own flowing script and then the large *D*, but here her hand had seemed to falter and the letter looked as though it might have been written by a child.

If he did nothing, he was telling himself as he stared at the spire of St. Patrick's in the rising storm, then this moment might pass. There must be some mistake. There had to be.

But like thunder from afar, other warnings now came to him: how hard it had been to get her on the telephone these last ten days, the apartment where she had not slept last night, and now . . . this.

He hated the sight of the rose on his desk. The silver box seemed an insult. He turned the card over and looked at it: a Park Avenue florist.

The pain struck again like a cancer, sharper, bending him over as it pierced through his gut.

When it passed, he sat back in his chair, stretching himself carefully. "Oh boy," he said in a kind of wonder. He tried to think rationally. He was an adult. He had had a new love affair. She had left him.

He breathed evenly, his lips compressed, and slowly whatever demons were waiting for him withdrew. He knew they weren't gone for long, or far, but they were gone for now. He'd accept that.

Tallulah came in. She closed the door behind her. "Look," she said, "I don't know what's happened but I'm here."

Jules stared at her without expression. The feeling that rose in him was anger at her. She had warned him. She had been right. A great fury seemed to break in him and he said nothing. He couldn't speak. If he did, he would regret whatever he said for a long time.

Tallulah nodded as though she understood and then she went out again, shutting the door very softly.

Jules spun around in his chair and looked out the gray window to where other buildings had become shadows in the rain, lights beckoning in the sky, other men working, women flirting, life going on.

"You are a child," he told himself severely.

He picked up the card from the florist and stared at the telephone. The doorman in the building, when he approached him that morning, had said with surprise, "Miss Martins left, Mr. Edwards." Jules could see as he spoke that he had thought Jules would know. Danielle and he had made no secret of their affair. Now, the whole building staff would know that Danielle had walked out.

Still Jules had had to force himself to ask, "When?"

The doorman shrugged, lifting the heavy braids on the shoulders of his uniform, and looked out into the wet morning, where schoolchildren were kicking sodden leaves in Riverside Park. "Two days ago," he said. "That singer came with her, and they cleaned out the apartment, and they left. Singer seemed real happy, real . . ." The doorman seemed to understand suddenly what the news of Tracy Harmon's happiness was doing to Jules. "I don't know, Mr. Edwards," the doorman said, closing up. "They just came, Miss Martins and that singer, and she said she was going to be gone for some time, told the desk and the super and they went off in a long car. Big car. Limousine."

A limousine. All the star trappings. The record was cut, the tracks laid down, and now all that had to be done was to have them "mixed," as the industry terminology went. Tracy Harmon wouldn't be needed, nor would Danielle.

And nor would Jules Edwards. He'd played his part. He'd kept everyone at bay until they got what they wanted.

Jules flipped the card onto his desk, where it spun away among his papers.

He could laugh, he thought, if he didn't feel so terrible. He tried letting the full force of his feelings in, the feelings he had been shutting out by keeping his mind absolutely blank ever since he'd dialed the telephone at his bedside that morning and it had rung and rung in Danielle's apartment down the hall; ever since he'd asked as casually as he could if the doorman had seen her. Even then he must have known, he thought now with a sigh; he must have felt the small dark cloud, almost a speck in the distance, that was approaching, pulling with it a whirlwind that would threaten to endanger his whole life.

Believe, he thought ironically, and the feelings overturned his heart, bringing nausea again.

Tallulah came in. She was carrying coffee on a tray. She had a list of his morning appointments neatly typed on Star Records letterhead paper. He liked to have it stuck in his blotter every morning so he could cast his eye down quickly and know how the day was moving.

Tallulah looked at the rose and then at his face. He didn't say anything. She left the coffee tray, put the sheet of paper in the corner of his blotter and went out.

The windows of the office misted over with the flashing storm. Jules felt shut in, trapped. He sat down behind his desk holding all his feelings at bay and placed his hands in a pyramid under his chin, swinging back and forth very slowly in his chair.

Danielle's face came to him—the two bright green eyes that opened wide in astonishment; the small perfect nose he would stroke with his finger when he'd lean close to whisper words that he hadn't said to anyone in a long time, some that he had never said at all; and the full, peach-blossom lips that parted as he spoke to her, ready, it always seemed, with their own vow before he had finished speaking.

The pain hit him as sharp as a knife and he closed his eyes and winced. His chest seemed to constrict and his breath caught in his throat. A wave of nausea passed over him, and he broke out in a damp sweat that seemed to ooze from his body as though a poison had struck.

"Oh God," he whispered to the ceiling

with his eyes still closed, a prayer for deliverance.

He didn't want to believe this. He refused. He would trust as he had told her she must trust. This was different, they were different, the future for them . . .

"You fool," he told himself, trying to steady the world that threatened to crumble about him.

It wouldn't happen this time. No, it would not happen this time.

Tallulah came in again. She shut the door behind her and looked at the silver box.

"Take it away," Jules said evenly.

"We're all family here," Tallulah told him.

"Yeah," Jules said without expression. Then he could smile, almost genuinely. "You ever let anyone know about this, Tallulah, I'll wring your neck," he said. There wasn't any joke in his voice. His voice was the voice of a dead man, an echo from some emotional grave where he felt himself sliding deeper into the earth.

"You want to tell me what happened out there?" she asked.

"No," he said.

He picked up the rose and looked at it. It was a nice rose, he thought. If she had written the card yesterday when he was on the way back, she might even still be here in the city. He dropped it into the box.

Tallulah said, "There might be some other explanation." She wasn't convinced, but she felt she had to say it.

"You want to try for some?" Jules asked. "I could use a laugh right now."

Right at that moment he had a flash of Danielle lying on the bed in the cabin in Santa Barbara, her long limbs tossed with the sheets. He had a flash of himself waking in the night, her fragrance mixing with his own, and he remembered the thought that had come to him, as real as it had been back then: Home, I'm home.

The pain came again, fiercely, but he fought it and it withdrew.

"Oh, baby," Tallulah said softly.

"Don't, Tallulah," Jules begged her, pain in his voice, anguish as his heart wrenched again. He couldn't feel this, he mustn't.

Tallulah withdrew back to the bounds that they both felt more comfortable. "You want me to hold calls?" she asked.

He looked at the list of people he expected to speak to that day. "No," he said firmly. "We go on."

"Good man," Tallulah said. Without asking, she reached for the silver box and took it and the rose out and closed the door behind her.

With the box gone, some air seemed to come into the room and Jules breathed more evenly. The rain fell heavily outside and the city was as dark as night. He found that he was dialing Danielle's number without any thought that he was going to, and this time a voice came on: "Service to this number has been discontinued. No further information is available." The voice went off and he was left with a humming sound.

Tallulah buzzed him. "Harry's on long distance," she said.

Jules pulled himself together. "All right, I'll take it," he said.

"Jesus you're at the desk early," Harry said.

What time was it in California? Jules thought. Eleven New York, eight California. Harry himself was one of the few who hit the office out there as near as he could to New York time.

"Couldn't sleep," Jules said. That was the truth. He had waited all night for some sound, the door, a sound in the hall. He had known, he told himself now; he must have. Something in Danielle's voice had told him that she was going. He could recall her now at the terminal in Los Angeles when she'd touched his cheek, looking deep into his eyes. She had known, but all of those feelings, the way their bodies seemed to meld together as one, the lovemaking that for Jules had seemed to promise a thousand times more happiness than he had ever thought possible, opening doors to fairy kingdoms long shut . . . was all that false?

"You there, Jules?"

"Sure, sure, Harry," Jules hastened to reassure him. "I'm here. Just . . . just tired," he ended lamely.

"Listen, boy," Harry told him. "You take that lady of yours and you go take some time off. You deserve it. You heard this last tape?"

For a second Jules couldn't think of what Harry was talking about. When he did, it came to him like a wave rising out of the sea in front of the *Sapphire*, threatening to capsize the boat: Harmon's tape. The last one, which had been cut the day before yesterday. Harry had it out there.

"No," Jules said.

"Dynamite! Gold—better, platinum," Harry said. "You can tell the kid he's a millionaire, Jules."

Jules's emotions seemed to steady at those words: a millionaire. More than that, a hundred million dollars, more than likely. People would do a lot for a hundred million dollars.

But though his mind seemed to suddenly fill with laughter, his heart stopped the laughter cold by bringing to him a floating froth of dark curls tossed by a warm breeze from the channel, and in his mind her face turned to look at him, open, honest . . .

"I'll do that, Harry," Jules said, trying to keep all emotion out of his voice.

"Give yourself a treat, Jules," Harry said in unconscious cruelty. "Go down into the studio; make them play you the tape. The guy's got the voice of an angel."

That somehow seemed perfect, and Jules laughed, but his voice betrayed him and choked, and Harry said, "Jules?"

"Something in my throat," Jules told him.

Harry wasn't convinced. "Listen to the tape, Jules," Harry said more slowly. "I want a Christmas release. This is the crossover we've been looking for. He's the new Sinatra; he'll take all of them, all of the generations. That's what they're saying out here."

"I'll do that, Harry," Jules told him. Then he lied. "Tallulah's walked in. I have to go, Harry. Meeting coming up."

"Okay." Jules could hear the concern in Harry's voice.

An angel, Jules thought, as he placed the receiver back. Had they planned it, the two of them, Danielle and Harmon? They couldn't have known that Harmon would deliver like this, Jules thought. And the apartment down the hall from him. That couldn't have been planned. That had to be coincidence. But you took your opportunities where you found them. He heard an echo in his mind of something else and at first he couldn't identify it. When he did, he laughed out loud, one long genuine laugh, the first that he had been able to come up with.

"You make contacts there," Beth's voice echoed out of the past, childlike, wheedling. And he remembered where they had been speaking of: They had been speaking of the old Studio 54 when it was more than just a dance hall, when it was full of names and stars and star makers.

"You know what they want?" he had argued with her, feeling their own relationship eroding in this endless round of good times.

"Sure I do," Beth had said, putting her hand flat on his chest and kissing him lightly on the chin. "But I'm not doing anything about it. They want to use me, and

I use them. I win. *You* and I win," she had hurried to add.

He could remember the conversation as clearly as if it had been last night. And her parting words, too: "Everybody uses everybody else."

His whole body now seemed to come together again, his mind and heart joined in a feeling of sadness that he could at least function with. His mind had been reeling off in great swings of disbelief followed by sudden anger at the betrayal, while his body was already ahead, feeling sick, upset, lost. But now it was one, like a condition of the flu that was constant but not enough to keep him away.

He could feel like this a long time, he thought.

So, he told himself, a New York story.

He had come along and they had used him. Everybody uses everybody.

Another picture came to his mind: a man's wide back with a long fall of blond hair, and as it turned, Danielle's face raised to meet Tracy Harmon's lips as her own dark beauty was entwined with his.

"Don't do this to yourself, Jules," he told himself quietly, but the image held for one long second more before it faded as it would on a dark screen in a motion-picture theater.

He stood up. He felt like a sick man. His knees felt weak and he stood still until he was sure that he was in control of himself.

Tallulah knocked and came in. He turned to look at her. "You look like hell!" she said unsympathetically. Jules knew that she was using shock treatment, but still he was so angry that his feelings showed.

"Calls?" he asked.

She took her time to look him over, waiting for him to give her another opening, but when she saw he wouldn't, she handed him the morning's list. He picked up a pencil and numbered them. "Dial them," he told her. "I'll take them in that order."

She went out, and within a minute the first call came in. He sat in his chair, turning his mind to the business at hand, the business that, over the last years, he had learned to use to fortify his self-image, his sustenance when there was nothing else. He had seen land ahead and sailed toward it, his hopes rising that this was some unmarked paradise that men spoke of, and the land had faded, a mirage. The world was full of tales like that. He had an earlier one himself to add to it, if anyone should ever ask again. He had been a fool.

Slowly the pressure of the day, the details, took his full concentration and for a while he was lost in the world where he had spent all this time for years. The pain was there always, and if he so much as gave it a moment it struck, a viper curled within him, but he was too much a professional to allow it to ravage him today. He worked on through the morning, and then, when the calls died as the city went to lunch, he sat back, his desk a field of yellow sheets filled with the tiny script he used to make his notations from his calls.

Nothing—an emotional emptiness and an exhaustion at the long night flight, the sleeplessness and the day's work.

The pain would come again, he knew that; but if he could drive it back today, he could be sure of victory eventually.

Tallulah came in. "Food?"

"No," he said.

He patted his stomach. "Don't need it." And then came the first of many small recollections that would rise within him. He remembered standing naked in front of the mirror in the Beverly Hills Hotel, looking at his own strong, dark body and thinking that he would be watching it age beside Danielle's own perfect figure, the slow changes a gift of love to each other, records of time passed and enjoyed, not the sad, fearful loss he saw in all his single friends who strained to keep their figures in some desperate competition with younger men.

Something of his distant thoughts must have shown in his eyes, for Tallulah collapsed in the chair across from his desk. She seldom took liberties like that. They had a carefully worked-out relationship of their own.

"I'm going to be all right," he told her, speaking dispassionately. He tipped back and put his hands behind his head, his feet on the desk.

"Okay, honey," Tallulah said.

"You can say it if you want."

"I wouldn't," she said. She looked down into the handkerchief she was carrying, and Jules thought that maybe she had been crying.

He thought to ask her about herself. "You fine, Tallulah?" he asked.

She looked up quickly. "Yes," she said. "Why?"

He indicated the handkerchief.

She picked it up and stuffed it into the sleeve of her purple dress. "Oh, Jules," she said, "I'm so sorry."

"You warned me," he said.

Neither of them spoke for a while and the rain ran down the outside of the window. Outside the storm clouds obscured everything else in the city.

"Damn fools, aren't we?" he said to her.

The desk was between them. "Well," Tallulah said uncertainly, looking first at the carpet, "I guess we still feel; that's the problem."

They were trying to find some language to say what had to be said, but they had lived here in this city, in this business long enough to find the very words unworthy. He should have known better. They both knew that. And even knowing better, he still felt this deep unseen gash within that was widening even as he tried to lose it.

"Nothing would help, would it?" she said.

He gave her a half smile. "No." Then after a second he said apologetically, almost in shame, "I had forgotten how much it could hurt."

Now he managed a small laugh and Tallulah looked up, uncertain of how to respond.

"Don't worry," he told her. "I'm going to be fine."

"Yes," she said, and she reached for the handkerchief. She drew a deep breath. Maybe everybody was transparent, Jules thought. Maybe we all thought we had all these secrets and we didn't: The world could see right through us. Tallulah knew what had happened; he was sure of that. And not just the details of how Danielle had used him to buy time for Tracy Harmon. That was clear as day and would be all over the industry within the week.

Believe. The word struck him like a knife.

He said, "You're a good dear friend, Tallulah."

She rose, knowing that their time was over. "Calls?" she asked.

He nodded, and he could see that she was relieved. She was a good dear friend, he told himself for the second time. He was a lucky man in many, many ways.

Still he felt sick throughout his whole body, but at least his mind was clearing.

And he had another feeling now: anger. The rose in the box. He tossed aside the yellow pages that were still scattered across the desk until he found the small card: "Forgive me," she had written.

The hatred came so swiftly that his sight blurred, and when he came back to the moment he was shaking with rage.

"Forgive me."

And somewhere in him, for the second time today, an old proverb rose out of his memory. "Nothing is unforgivable except deliberate cruelty."

All right, for God's sake, he said to himself, but his fingers still shook when he dropped the card in the wastebasket.

Children asked for forgiveness. They sat

on their daddy's laps and said, "Forgive me," and it was over.

Children. He had been thinking that the first day he saw her. He had been thinking that he was too old to be raising children, thinking that Tracy Harmon would no doubt be a child and he, Jules, would have to be the stern parent.

The calls started to come in and he took them and his own world closed about him again. He would think of all this later, he thought, and the afternoon drew out while the city outside reluctantly came to an early night as the storm rose, whipping winds about the tallest buildings, wailing of the winter yet to come.

Jules was exhausted when Tallulah came in. She looked worn herself. "Hey," he said. "You should have gone."

"Oh," she said, lifting one broad shoulder, "you know how it is; the walk home seems longer in the dark."

She seemed to hear what she had said. But there wasn't any taking the words back. She said, "You want a drink?"

"I want to go home to my own apartment and get a decent night's sleep," Jules said, putting a good front on it. He knew exactly what she meant about the walk being longer in the dark.

She didn't pry. She didn't push. He heard

her go out. He wanted to get drunk; he wanted to be somewhere else. He wanted . . . those were a child's wants. This was real life. This was where he lived, where he worked.

He could feel the feelings reaching for him. He rose and took his coat off the tall stand near the door, closed the door behind him and went down in the elevator with a group of unspeaking businessmen. Once through the lobby he felt safe out in the cold, wet night, the wind coming down Fifth Avenue with a passion of its own.

He saw a cab with its light on and signaled it down. Inside he held on to his briefcase as though he had the secrets to the discovery of penicillin in it. His hands shook whenever they were free. His body was telling him he was a fraud, his heart dropping away as though an aircraft had fallen a hundred feet beneath him. His brow was sweating.

The cab driver looked at him in the mirror. "Not well, buddy?" he asked.

"Flu," he said.

"Lot of it going around," the driver said. "I blame the Russians."

The driver had a theory that took the rest of the journey to propound. Jules handed him the closest he could come to the fare and left more than two dollars tip. The night air made his stomach roll with nausea and he went quickly through the lobby, which seemed to have been relit like a stadium in his absence; but he knew it was just that the light was unnaturally bright to him.

The hallway stretched like a sprinting track. He couldn't get the key in the lock at first, and then once in, he slammed the door behind him as though the demons he had feared earlier were real and they were after him.

He dropped his coat on the floor and went to sit on the windowsill looking down at the river. He had separated from his body, he felt, was floating above it, looking down at this spoiled man, this man-child, feeling a pain because he had been hurt, a pain he should have been prepared for. The spirit that floated above had no sympathy for the man sitting in the dark. None. He should have known better. That was running in the fast track, real life.

The man on the windowsill could hear the accusations being thrown at him. He accepted them. He knew it was all true. But he could feel the movement within him of feelings that he had treasured, the touch of her skin, the way she had looked at him in the dark when all they seemed to need to do was face each other, no word ever possible to express the emotion that passed like a current between them. The man on the windowsill still held to those feelings, and because he did, the pain came in as real as the pain of childhood and he began to cry, quietly, so quietly no one would ever know. He cried for himself, and he cried for Danielle, and then he just cried, silently and for a long time, glad that no one would ever know his pain as he finally bid farewell to his own last dreams, the most fragile ones, the ones that could only be woven between two people and even then only by two people who believed in dreams.

After a lot of time had passed, he stood up and looked about his apartment and the pieces of his life seemed to come into focus. The room steadied and he saw that nothing had really changed: Here was the life he had been living before, the stage ready for him again.

He was tired, and he dropped his clothes in the living room, pulling them off as though they had had something to do with what had happened. When he went into the bedroom he was naked. His skin was cold and he crawled into bed, curling up as he hadn't in years, and dropped into an immediate sleep. When he woke with his heart pounding it was from a dream of falling from the deck of the *Sapphire* and losing height into a blue sea that got darker and darker.

Something woke him later in the night. At first he couldn't identify it; then he realized that it was the faint smell of lavender on his pillow. He sat up and pulled the pillow slip off and dropped it over the side of the bed.

Still, when he lay down the lavender was there again, and he realized that the sheets, the pillow cases were fresh. The maid would have changed them. The lavender was in the very pillow itself. He pushed it aside, and then slowly he reached for it again. He cradled the pillow to him, and after some time his mind released his body to another sleep and in this sleep Danielle was back in his arms, her firm flesh back under his, her lips reaching for his, and they met in a fiery passion that made promises to each other that no words would ever make as their bodies closed about one another, hungry with an appetite that wouldn't be denied.

The dream passed and Jules slept on, and when he awoke he was more tired than he had ever been in his life.

He watched the sky gray into morning, then called the office. "Tell Harry I'm going south to the boat," he told Tallulah.

"Yes," she said.

"If you need me . . ."

"Go, Jules," she said. "Go."

Chapter Eleven

The bow rose to greet the pounding wave and the spray blinded Jules. He closed his eyes to let the worst of the wave fall behind the *Sapphire* and opened them to look directly into the burning disk of the sun.

The world was a place of blazing light that became shadows as he changed the direction of the *Sapphire* and the white sails hid the sun.

He could feel the spray drying in the warm Caribbean heat. His skin was taut with the sun and the sea, and his body strong from ten days alone on the boat.

He tied the tiller, holding the *Sapphire* to her course southward, and moved quickly down into the cabin. Sailors were meant to be tidy, he knew, but all about him was the clutter of his flight from New York. He had gone to the airport with just his duffel bag and what he wore and had stepped off the flight in St. Thomas four hours later into a world that was slower, more brightly colored and unaware of his pain.

The heavy tropical air had seemed fresher to him than the air of any mountaintop, and as he stood on the dock a half hour later, the sight of the *Sapphire* anchored out in the bay had brought to him a moment of joy that waved a banishing hand back at the demons he had left behind.

The two youngsters who had brought the boat down stood, sunburned and innocent in their ragged cutoffs, grinning their open sailor's grins at him, waiting for his response. "She looks fine," he told them.

"She's a natural, Mr. Edwards," the older of the boys said. "She could sail *herself* down, I tell you. You going to want a crew to take her home in spring?"

Jules grinned. "Maybe," he said. "If I do, you'll be it."

"Great," they both said.

He was in a hurry to set foot on the *Sapphire*. His blue tropic-weight blazer felt like a costume, and his toes crawled in his dark loafers to be free. The younger boy took him out to the boat.

The dinghy bumped gently against the dark hull of the razor-slim sailboat. "Man," the boy said. "If I could think of one reason for the nine-to-five, this lady would be it." He patted the hull.

"There are other ways to make a living," Jules said, trying to do what he could to help the boy understand what his father probably wanted for him.

"You don't miss her?" the boy asked curiously as he hefted Jules's single canvas bag onto the deck.

"You want a secret?" Jules asked.

"Sure."

"Every day," Jules said. "Sometimes I think maybe you and Jack out there"—he pointed off across the water toward the boy's buddy—"may have the right idea."

The boy nodded. "I'll leave you the dinghy," he said. He dove overboard and stroked his way to shore.

Jules went below and threw his duffel bag on the bunk in the forward cabin. The *Sapphire* rocked slightly under him and he sat down on the edge of the bunk. His mind was blank, deliberately so. He stared at the mahogany walls of the cabin, walls of workmanship that couldn't be duplicated any

longer. People didn't do work like that anymore. There was a small scratch on one of
the lower panels. He would fix that himself
this trip.

This trip. The words stood out in his
mind. *This trip.* Danielle's face appeared
in his mind, distant, mocking. This was to
be their trip.

Impatient with himself, he threw off his
blazer, stripped down and pulled out a pair
of shorts from his duffel bag.

On deck, he felt the immediate sting of
the hot sun on his skin. He drew a deep
breath and dove overboard as the boy had.
He stroked hard around the *Sapphire* a half
dozen times and climbed back up the rope
ladder.

Shaking the water from his hair, he felt
his head clearing as it hadn't in months,
details fleeing before the fresh smell of the
sea breeze and the movement of the tide.

The sun was sinking lower above the
island town. The palm trees were darkly
laced against the paler rise of the distant
mountains. Jules went below and found the
boys had stocked up the *Sapphire* with
provisions as he had instructed them by
cable.

He went back on deck, his skin dry from
the tropic heat, and sat there cross-legged
until the first lights came on in the small

town. The breeze was rising and the tall mast of the *Sapphire* rolled in an arc above. The master was on board; she was anxious to be gone. He watched while other lights came on in the few sailboats scattered about the bay, and he could feel the tension unlock from his muscles.

The sky became a midnight blue, then a black like jeweler's velvet starred with pure white diamonds.

Jules rose and set his own running lights, red for starboard, green for port. From across the water a steel band began to play light tropical music and he heard the peal of laughter from a nearby yacht.

Alone he hand-cranked the anchor on board and secured it. The wind was stronger now, much stronger, promising a good run to open sea. He unfurled the sails, letting them flap loose into the breeze, and then barefoot he padded about the boat, who knew she was to sail, her deck rising and falling in an excitement that was almost animal.

Jules brewed himself a cup of strong coffee in the galley, tore the cellophane wrapping from a cigar and went on deck. He set his lines, pulling the sails taut, and the *Sapphire* bucked wildly under his hand as he set her course for the harbor mouth. The sails filled with wind and he settled back into the open cockpit as the large graceful craft slowly came to full power, slicing through the water as the dark headland passed on his right and the spangled lights of the small town dropped behind to the left, the music trailing after the *Sapphire* until that too was lost on the wind.

The night was clear and dark, the sea strong and the *Sapphire* sure. Jules sat back alone in his own world, heading for the open sea and a new dawn.

Chapter Twelve

*J*ules laid his charts out on the map table and drew a red line toward the distant island. A strange place for a charter party to ask to be picked up. Most of them flew into St. Thomas, where they could do a day's shopping and partying before they came on board.

He shrugged. In nine months of chartering the *Sapphire,* he'd learned that there was no use second-guessing human nature. He'd seen them all: the overweight business executives and their whinnying wives, the shy honeymooners, the heavy drinking parties of only men all determined to outfish their buddies though their eyes were half-crossed most of the time from booze. And the good ones too: the ones who behaved liked guests and let him put the *Sapphire* through her paces for them while they enjoyed the ever-present sun, the warm days and clear nights.

He wondered what it would be this time. He was to meet the party at an almost unmarked island at the end of the Bahamian chain. He opened the hidden gun locker and checked that both the rifle and the handgun were there and loaded. The Caribbean was infested with pirates these days, many of them searching for a single-crewed seaworthy vessel. They would board one if they could, kill the skipper and use the boat for a single drug run before sinking her in the open sea.

The money for this charter was excellent, almost too good to be true. Jules was suspicious as soon as he got the radio dispatch in St. Barts. Under most circumstances he would have turned it down, all his antennae warning him to stay away, but the funds were low. He'd only taken on the minimum charters for the last nine months and his own cash backup was almost exhausted.

The *Sapphire* was the finest mistress a man could want, but she was expensive.

Now that there was no more money coming regularly from Star Records, Jules had to learn to do all the maintenance himself. He loved it. He didn't regret his decision for a minute, but charter boating was a hard way to make a living.

Popeye, the one-eyed ship's cat who had joined the crew of the *Sapphire* at Grenada without invitation on Jules's first solo voyage, came out from his sleeping place in the bow and rubbed against Jules's leg. "Another charter, Popeye," Jules told him.

Popeye arched his back disdainfully and raised the fur along his hackles.

"Oh, don't be so judgmental," Jules told him with a laugh. "They may be just fine."

Popeye shook himself as if to dismiss any possibility that landlubbers would pass his muster. Popeye liked the open sea, the *Sapphire* and Jules. He had heard all Jules's problems on the first voyage when Jules had thought his heart would break in two. He had listened silently while he lay on the deck watching for flying fish to rise out of the sea in silver arcs and flop on the deck at the heartless mercy of Popeye's sharp claws.

Nothing could surprise Popeye.

Jules made himself some strong coffee and went on deck. The *Sapphire* held the wind, sails full as she pushed through a slow sea toward the speck of an island lost in the open, sun-bright sea.

Jules lay back with the sun on his face. He had changed in nine months. He was leaner, his body burned nearly mahogany from daily work in the open. He had accepted his self-chosen destiny and he had no regrets.

He closed his eyes and listened to Popeye purring nearby. The dreams still came sometimes. Not as often as they had at first, when he would wake with his heart pounding, a great, nameless fear pushing through him, and the sheets soaked with sweat.

He would lay in the dark and her face would slowly fade from his dream, the emerald eyes going last, mocking him as they finally blinked closed and he was alone again in the dark.

There had been times then when he thought foolish thoughts, fatal thoughts, his mind a place of confusion where every decision seemed huge, the smallest of as much import as the greatest, and sometimes he had had to take the *Sapphire* into some small deserted cove and drop anchor because he was unsure of his own captaining.

Days would pass while he caught his own fish, swimming deep among the reefs with the spear gun, hoping to exhaust himself with sheer physical work so that when night came and the trade winds rose and he was alone again with only Popeye as his companion, he might finally sleep.

He had cabled Star Records after the first week, saying that he needed an indefinite leave, and something must have passed between Tallulah and Harry for the message came back, "Take your time. All the best. Harry."

He had taken his time; more than that, he had lost track of time. He blamed Popeye for that and loved him for it too, for Popeye had slapped Jules's eighteen-hundred-dollar watch overboard with one swift movement of his paw as the *Sapphire* rose high on a strong sea and both of Jules's hands were more than occupied with the wheel and the rigging. He had seen the gold watch spin out of the cockpit and drop like a Spanish doubloon into a storm-black sea, and he had cursed the ragged one-eyed cat.

He tried counting the days after that, marking them on a sheet of paper above the map table, but one day he forgot and soon the passing of the days became unimportant. He knew what week it was within a day or two, and that, along with the weather, which he had learned to read from the movement of the clouds and the flight of the seabirds toward land when trouble was brewing, seemed sufficient for any man.

The second cable to Star, resigning, had brought a veritable windfall of cables back, including one that offered Jules more money than he had ever expected to earn in a lifetime. But by then the decision was made. He didn't know when it had been made, but it had been, and he knew it because he finally felt at home. The *Sapphire* had become his home.

Peace came more slowly, the dreams refusing to leave his life as the gold watch had, dropping overboard and leaving him to a new time, a new pace. She still haunted him with her emerald eyes and her perfect lips that sometimes seemed to be speaking to him, but the words were lost when he awoke and he learned not to strain to hear them.

On nights when he couldn't sleep at all, he sat on deck looking into the dark at the horizons of his chosen world and he knew he was lonely but he knew that that was any man's lot and he knew that one day he would learn to live with that loneliness.

"Okay, Popeye," Jules told his old companion now. "We stock up in Nassau and then go south."

That would mean making a detour from the red-lined course he'd marked on the

chart. Jules went on deck and reset the
sails, heading into the sunset that washed
across the whole sky to the west, gold
and pink and turquoise, promising perfect
weather for the morrow. He set the *Sapphire* on her course and, as night fell, withdrew to the cabin after a light meal, falling
into the sleep that now came more easily,
one ear cocked for trouble—the straining of
a rigging line, the touch of danger along the
mahogany hull of the boat.

He awoke before dawn to a silk green sky
with shredded pink cloud scattering ahead
of a gentle wind. Dawn brought the islands
on the horizon, and soon he was passing
into the harbor ahead of the customs
launch, his yellow immigration flag raised.
The *Sapphire* was a known sight by now,
and Jules was trusted. The formalities took
less than half an hour and he was soon
ordering enough provisions for his charter
party, which he would meet that night in
the south. The market was a place of laughter, dark skins, the vivid colors of tropical
fruit, the dangling silver flesh of new-
caught fish.

He was out of the harbor, the *Sapphire*
fully provisioned, by evening, sailing into a
red sky where the stars already burned like
rubies as they cried out the coming night.

A crescent moon cast its path on the

water, leading the *Sapphire* south, and Popeye, awake for once, sat on the bow looking forward with his single good eye as though he expected to find some lost treasure of his own.

Jules furled the sails and went below, leaving a sea anchor to drag behind to slow the *Sapphire*, but that night sleep wouldn't come and his heart beat with a long-forgotten trouble, bringing to his restless mind a picture of a hillside and an inn, a woman who lay against him with her lavender-fragrant hair pressed against his cheek and then later, when he dropped into a moment's sleep, another dream, this time of firelight on rose pink flesh and his own voice choked in his throat as two arms that were then as familiar as his own held him to her, crying out his name.

He awoke and went on deck, buttoning an old yellow flannel shirt loosely over his faded jeans, pulled in the sea anchor and raised the sails. Popeye watched him un-blinkingly from the bow, a grave expression on his old cat's face.

The islands were dark lines against the dawn-gray horizon as the crescent moon faded into a sky that burned to the blue of a seabird's egg, then darker with a full fiery sun rising out of the east, whitening everything except the waves that tossed in gleaming masses about the *Sapphire*'s hull as she pushed forward. The *Sapphire* had a mind of her own today, bucking fretfully.

A flock of seabirds came out to greet the boat, moving in circles about the full white sails and crying their welcome.

The island grew to a jade green slope rising from the blue ocean. Jules could make out a scattering of wooden huts above a tiny harbor, and sticking into the sea, an airstrip on a golden spur of land.

He dropped one sail, and the *Sapphire* lowered herself comfortably into the welcoming sea. A reef, half-hidden below the surface of the water, lined the blue with white. Jules tacked to starboard, bringing the elegant form of his boat around, and there directly ahead of him was the tiny seaport that was his destination.

He took down all the sails and brought the *Sapphire* expertly to the old dock that stood on sturdy pylons in the gem-clear water. Two young, black native boys took hold of the lines he threw, laughing bright, white smiles at him, and soon the *Sapphire* was docked.

No one came to greet him. The airstrip out beyond the town was deserted except for an unpainted wooden shack and a flagpole with an old-fashioned wind sleeve attached.

He stepped ashore and looked about. Further up the waterfront an open café seemed to be the only restaurant. He had been warned to provision in Nassau. The island was, he had been told, only a scattering of fishing shacks.

The noon sun cast shadows across the dusty street as Jules lazily walked barefoot toward the café. The charter passengers obviously hadn't arrived. The café owners would know everything, as they did at all the waterfronts of the Caribbean.

A dog came out to greet him, barking ferociously, then lost interest in the intense heat and flopped over in the nearest shade, his tail giving one last weak greeting before he closed his eyes.

Jules saw her in the deepest shade thrown by the thatched awning that stuck out from the café.

His heart stopped and his body went as cold as ice in the Caribbean sun. She was seated, looking away toward the inland part of the island where the land sloped up toward what once must have been a volcano mouth and now was draped in thick vegetation, banana trees and vines and creepers that stained the highest peaks with red flowers.

He knew she had seen him dock. He knew as clearly as though she had called his name that she knew he was watching her.

And now she turned slowly and looked at him, and the emerald eyes burned from under the shadow of the awning, bright, alluring, as vivid as the first time he had seen her in the doorway of her apartment.

The anger came then, rushing through him, and an emotion he had forgotten in his new life, a fierce hatred that burned out of him as his mouth set. He wanted to turn and walk back to the *Sapphire* without a word, but his arms, strong with half-year's work at sea, had tautened in rage and he wanted to reach for her, reach for her, and . . .

His heart wouldn't slow. He heard a sound and looked down to see Popeye, who made a rule of never leaving the boat, walking carefully up the sandy street. The dog raised his head in disbelief and half rose to his haunches before dropping back again into his siesta.

The world seemed to have frozen about Jules, all movement slow, the sun golden above, each leaf of every nearby vine exactly etched, and there in the shade, rising to her feet, was Danielle.

His breath came back to him. The shadows fled. He could hear the clucking of hens behind the small restaurant, the noises of the owners inside. A child cried out in laughter and the two black boys who had helped tie up the *Sapphire* raced up to Jules, holding out their hands. He looked away from Danielle as she came toward him out of the shelter of the thatched awning, and he dug into his pockets for coins for the boys. When he had paid them, she was standing looking at him from half a dozen feet away.

The shock was that she was exactly as he remembered her. But there was more: She was beautiful with her gemstone eyes, the shining fall of dark curls, the skin that had been out of the sun for as long as his had been under it while he'd fled from exactly this memory. But he had forgotten the curve of her hips as she stood facing him; the way, when she moved, she gave some special grace to movements that were no different from any other woman's movements, a grace that was all her own. Against his will, his heart brought back to him all the longing, all the loss.

He blinked and hoped that when he opened up his eyes he would find that some perverse trick of memory had conjured her up.

But when he opened his eyes into the glaring light of the noon sun, she was still there.

"Tricks," he said, and his voice was sad with the recalled knowledge of the past.

She blinked as though he had struck her.

"Jules," she said, her voice soft, the voice from the past, the voice that had whispered to him in shadowed rooms, words spoken so close to his ears that they might have been echoes of his own dreams. "Please . . ."

"What could you possibly want from me now?" he asked, not looking at her.

His body had broken out in a sweat that was as icy as the deepest sea.

"You were hard to find," she said.

He stared directly at her. He hoped that his eyes would tell her all she needed to know, and now she blinked in her own turn and looked at her feet and he had a moment to see her as she was, without the shock that had overcome him when he discovered whom he had been sent to meet. She was thinner, he saw. Her white cotton jeans were belted at her hips with a mauve scarf, and her blouse, pale blue and faded from a hundred washings, was wrinkled with the wear of her flight down.

Nothing could disguise that full body. As the moment stretched out, he could remember every inch of it, his own body bringing back scents and touches that he had long tried to forget.

"I don't want anything," she said, looking

at him. "I came to see you. I came to explain."

"You owe me nothing," Jules said. It was like a slap in the face.

Jules felt ashamed at the feelings that rose in him: the desire to hurt her. He looked about him and he thought, Children's games. And he remembered the first day he had met her, facing himself in the mirror and thinking he was too old to raise children.

"I owe you something . . . ," he began.

"Don't," she begged, and she looked down at her hands. "Please don't do this."

"Why not?" he asked. "If it hadn't been for you, I wouldn't have come here to the boat and started a new life. I guess you could say," he said with a bitter laugh, "that *you* gave me a new life. You and Harmon," he said, pushing home a last thrust of hatred.

She went white. She didn't look at him, didn't speak. The colors all about her pulsed in the hot afternoon air, the leaves of the bougainvillea, the mottled greens of the distant mountains, the red-gold sun in the fierce blue sky.

A small lizard crept out of the shade and stood looking up at them, from one to the other, its throat pulsing.

"I'm not taking you out on the *Sapphire*,"

he said, staring down the sun-bleached road to where the boat moved with the tide against the dock. "You can forget that."

Danielle looked down at her hands. "I just wanted to get time to speak to you," she said.

"Money wouldn't be any object," he said thoughtfully, looking to the airstrip. "You can go where you want, can't you? I heard the record was a big hit."

"Yes," she murmured.

"What do you want now?" he asked, the anger back. "Absolution?"

The fire that flared in her eyes brought back other emotions, which flamed through his limbs, so that he had to look away quickly lest he betray himself to her. Popeye sat watching them from across the sun-bright road, one unblinking eye fixed on Jules.

"I wanted to tell you I love you," Danielle Martins said evenly.

His first reaction was to want to laugh, but even that sound wouldn't rise in him. And then something else happened, something worse. He felt his heart lurch in his chest, begging him to believe her. He kept his head averted, facing Popeye, who wouldn't take his single eye off Jules, and the silence of the day was filled with the small, unheard sounds of the nearby jungle and the air with the sweet, beguiling odors of rot and freshly bloomed flowers.

When he turned to face her he must have shown some of the warring emotions in his own sun-lined face, for her next words were slower. "I do," she said.

He narrowed his eyes, trying to remember what it was about those two words that they had haunted his dreams. And then it came back, the time they had walked the beach in Santa Barbara together and the hawks had ridden the wind currents above and he had vowed to himself silently that she would one day speak those words to him.

"I loved you," he said now, but his words were merely echoes. He spoke in a type of wonder, remembering another time. "I loved you. You knew that. And you walked out."

She looked down at her hands again. The light in the rich mass of her hair taunted him and he wanted to reach for her and stroke it.

"Jules," she said, her voice breaking as she looked up at him, "he was my half brother."

The words hung there, and Jules could make no sense of them.

"It was his last chance and he was my half brother."

Finally something of what she was saying came through to Jules. "Tracy Harmon?" he said, his own words soft in the breath-catching heat of the tropical afternoon.

Danielle nodded without looking at him. "The first tapes were terrible," she said.

From the long-distant past, Jules could vaguely remember Tallulah's words that the first tapes were flat, unexceptional.

"He wanted it so badly," Danielle said, and now she was crying. "He was so young and he wanted it so badly and if he didn't get it . . ." Her voice trailed off into the silence.

Now Jules blinked and looked off past the *Sapphire* to the open sea. That world seemed so far, far away. The boy had been young, he remembered that, of course, and he could remember telling Danielle that this was Tracy Harmon's last chance at the brass ring. The desperation of the young and talented. That all looked so futile here with the boat ready to take him away from the island, the sun to warm him, the sea to provide. But it came back slowly, some of it: the desperation and the hunger, the feeling that life had no meaning if you couldn't make it to the top in this business, this *one* business.

Still when he looked at Danielle, who was facing him waiting for his judgment, he saw a stranger. His arms wanted to reach for her, his mouth to touch hers, his thighs to brush again against hers.

"You could have told me," he said.

She shook her head. "I nearly did. When we were in Santa Barbara. But you kept pressing me so hard. You seemed so *sure* of what you wanted for us and I got frightened. I kept thinking that I would tell you soon, even after I got back to New York. But by the time I wanted to, something else had happened. Tracy had started to play the final tapes, and though they were good, I knew something terrible was happening to him. I could see it in his eyes."

Jules remembered the final tapes. "The voice of an angel," Harry and Tallulah had said.

Danielle looked directly at Jules. "I didn't know until I got back to New York that he was still on drugs. . . ."

The voice of an angel.

Jules felt exhausted. He wanted to close his eyes and sleep. He wanted to wake with the fresh, clean sea about him and the sky above him cloudless. He heard Danielle's voice as though from a great distance.

"I took him away when the tapes were finished. I was frightened. I wrote you all about it, but all my letters came back." She wasn't apologizing anymore. She was just stating a fact.

"I had given instructions that nothing was to be forwarded," Jules said dully across the abyss between them. He could hear a ringing in his ears. He shook his head. Popeye sat unmoving. Jules looked dumbly at Danielle. Now that his heart had steadied, his mind seemed blank.

"I wanted you to know," she whispered.

She blinked then, closed her eyes for a long moment and opened them again very slowly as though she were afraid of the light. "He's gone," she said.

Again Jules seemed to have lost his bearings. He looked automatically to the sky, where at night alone on the boat he followed the stars to his destination, wherever it was. But the sky was white and hot and without answers.

"Tracy?" he said, hoping that he was wrong.

She couldn't bring herself to answer him. The breath left her body in a long wracking shudder. "I thought . . . ," she said, and her voice had dropped to a whisper, "that it had happened again."

She stopped. Jules's heart was in his throat. He wanted to reach for her but she looked so fragile, so lost in her own inner world, that he was afraid that if he reached for her she would crumble before him into dust.

When she started to speak again, her voice was as soft as the wind in the dust at their feet. "I came back and saw how Tracy was and I remembered my mother." She looked at Jules as though she were trying hard to remember something. "I never told you about her," she said.

"She wanted to be a dancer," he said quietly. "I remember that."

Danielle nodded slowly. "But there was more," she said. "I wasn't hiding anything from you. I just didn't want it to be part of our lives. You were so *sure*," she said, and it was an accusation, "and I trusted you, so I wanted it so desperately to be true." She had to stop before she went on. "When my father died, she remarried and Tracy was born. She tried to make Tracy everything she hadn't been, everything I had disappointed her by not being. They were . . . they were like a brother and sister, the two of them, even when he was a little child. They would dance together and sing and she always spoke as though they would be together forever. It was . . . unnatural, eerie to watch, and then one day we began to realize that she was . . . gone. Not dead. She was there in body but her spirit was gone. She spoke of things that had happened years ago as though they were happening today, and it got worse and worse, particularly for Tracy."

Now Danielle stopped and she drew herself up. Jules could see the anger throb in her. *"He was just a little boy.* He didn't know what was happening or what had been done to him, and when they took her away he cried and cried and cried and no one could ever explain to him that his mother was sick. They put her in a hospital and she died there."

"Danielle . . . ," Jules murmured, anxious to spare her the pain.

But she wouldn't be stopped. "Then it was up to me to look after him. All those songs he could sing and make so special . . ."

The voice of an angel.

". . . those were all sung to his mother. All of them. And finally he couldn't carry the burden any longer. I came back from Santa Barbara and saw what was happening and I couldn't think of anything except that it was happening again . . . and I took him away . . . but . . ."

Now Jules needed to hear it. "But what?" he asked quietly.

"But I couldn't save him," she said, and she began to cry. "He escaped me one day and then they called . . . and . . . he was gone."

Jules closed the gap between them and lifted her into his arms. "I love you," he said. His lips reached for hers, brushed against them like the soft touch of bougainvillea petals. He put his arm around her and they walked toward the boat, their bodies feeling the nearness of each other, and as they reached the boat he swept her into his arms and carried her on board.

She clung to him like a swimmer who has been alone in the sea too long. As he carried her down into the cabin his lips touched hers, and they were warm and hungry. He took her forward into his cabin and placed her gently on the wide bunk. Her eyes were gleaming with a mixture of tears and desire as he put his hand on the faded blue blouse and slowly undid the buttons, exposing her flesh to him as he lay beside her. Her arms wrapped around his neck and they explored each other's lips and mouths fiercely first, then more slowly, and finally, as the afternoon sun cast shadows across the island, they undressed each other with sure fingers until they lay against each other, flesh to flesh.

"I love you," she breathed in his ear, holding on to him. "I always will."

And their bodies found each other again,

touching familiar places, lost travelers coming across welcome places that slowly led them home, holding each other, calling out sounds in their own familiar language, until they both fell asleep, once again safe in each other's arms forever.

Enjoy romance and passion, larger-than-life...

Now, thrill to 4 Silhouette Intimate Moments novels (a $9.00 value)— ABSOLUTELY FREE!

If you want more passionate sensual romance, then Silhouette Intimate Moments novels are for you!

In every 256-page book, you'll find romance that's electrifying...involving... and intense. And now, these larger-than-life romances can come into your home every month!

4 FREE books as your introduction.

Act now and we'll send you four thrilling Silhouette Intimate Moments novels. They're our gift to introduce you to our convenient home subscription service. Every month, we'll send you four new Silhouette Intimate Moments books. Look them over for 15 days. If you keep them, pay just $9.00 for all four. Or return them at no charge.

We'll mail your books to you *as soon as they are published.* Plus, with every shipment, you'll receive the Silhouette Books Newsletter absolutely free. *And Silhouette Intimate Moments is delivered free.*

Mail the coupon today and start receiving Silhouette Intimate Moments. Romance novels for women...not girls.

Silhouette Intimate Moments

If you've enjoyed this book, mail this coupon and get 4 thrilling

Silhouette Desire®
novels FREE (a $7.80 value)

If you've enjoyed this Silhouette Desire novel, you'll love the 4 <u>FREE</u> books waiting for you! They're yours as our gift to introduce you to our home subscription service.

Get Silhouette Desire novels
before they're available anywhere else.

Through our home subscription service, you can get Silhouette Desire romance novels regularly—delivered right to your door! Your books will be *shipped to you two months before they're available anywhere else*—so you'll never miss a new title. Each month we'll send you 6 new books to look over for 15 days, without obligation. If not delighted, simply return them and owe nothing. Or keep them and pay only $1.95 each. There's no charge for postage or handling. And there's no obligation to buy anything at any time. You'll also receive a subscription to the Silhouette Books Newsletter *absolutely free!*

So don't wait. To receive your four FREE books, fill out and mail the coupon below *today!*

SILHOUETTE DESIRE and colophon are registered trademarks and a service mark of Simon & Schuster, Inc.

Silhouette Desire,® 120 Brighton Road, P.O. Box 5020, Clifton, NJ 07015

Yes, please send me FREE and without obligation, 4 exciting Silhouette Desire books. Unless you hear from me after I receive them, send me 6 new Silhouette Desire books to preview each month before they're available anywhere else. I understand that you will bill me just $1.95 each for a total of $11.70—with no additional shipping, handling or other hidden charges. **There is no minimum number of books that I must buy, and I can cancel anytime I wish.** The first 4 books are mine to keep, even if I never take a single additional book.

☐ Mrs. ☐ Miss ☐ Ms. ☐ Mr.   BDDLR4

Name	*(please print)*	

Address		Apt. #

City	State	Zip

| ( ) | | |
| Area Code | Telephone Number | |

Signature (If under 18, parent or guardian must sign.)

This offer, limited to one per household, expires June 30, 1985. Prices and terms subject to change. Your enrollment subject to acceptance by Simon & Schuster Enterprises

READERS' COMMENTS ON SILHOUETTE ROMANCES:

"I would like to congratulate you on the most wonderful books I've had the pleasure of reading. They are a tremendous joy to those of us who have yet to meet the man of our dreams. From reading your books I quite truly believe that he will someday appear before me like a prince!"
—L.L.*, Hollandale, MS

"Your books are great, wholesome fiction, always with an upbeat, happy ending. Thank you."
—M.D., Massena, NY

"My boyfriend always teases me about Silhouette Books. He asks me, how's my love life and naturally I say terrific, but I tell him that there is always room for a little more romance from Silhouette."
—F.N., Ontario, Canada

"I would like to sincerely express my gratitude to you and your staff for bringing the pleasure of your publications to my attention. Your books are well written, mature and very contemporary."
—D.D., Staten Island, NY

*names available on request